The Women Of Crooked Creek

A Collection of Four Short Works of Fiction

MK McClintock

Four courageous women, an untamed land, and the daring to embark on an unforgettable adventure.

The war is over between the North and the South, but the battles at home are just beginning. If you love stories of bravery and courage with unforgettable women and the men they love, you'll enjoy *The Women of Crooked Creek*.

Packsaddle
Press

Large Print Edition

Copyright © 2016 MK McClintock
2019 Large Print Paperback Edition
All rights reserved.

Packsaddle Press
Bigfork, Montana
cambronpublishing.com
mkmcclintock.com

The Women of Crooked Creek Copyright © 2016 MK McClintock
"Emma of Crooked Creek" Copyright © 2014 MK McClintock
"Hattie of Crooked Creek" Copyright © 2015 MK McClintock
"Briley of Crooked Creek" Copyright © 2015 MK McClintock
"Clara of Crooked Creek" Copyright © 2016 MK McClintock

"The Women of Crooked Creek"/MK McClintock
ISBN-13: 978-1733723237

Cover Design by MK McClintock

For the doers, dreamers, and adventurers who never give up. Continue to believe in yourself and reach for the stars.

TABLE OF CONTENTS

EMMA OF CROOKED CREEK

MK McCLINTOCK

The war is over between the North and the South, but the battles at home are just beginning.

Emma Hawkins is a dedicated doctor in the little town of Crooked Creek, Montana Territory. Casey Latimer is a wounded soldier in search of a new home and a new beginning. When Casey, battered and bruised, quite literally falls at Emma's feet, she is bound by duty to help him. What happens next is something Emma never expected.

EMMA OF CROOKED CREEK

Crooked Creek, Montana Territory
September 1865

THUNDER WOKE EMMA from the first decent night sleep she'd had in months. She looked around at the dark room. It wasn't the crash of thunder or even that grizzly her neighbor swore she saw last week. The front door of the one-room cabin reverberated as the pounding continued.

Emma reached for her husband's old Colt Navy Revolver, the only thing he'd left behind when he went to fight and die in the war. Her husband had taught her how to use the pistol on the long wagon ride out west, but only small critters ever saw the bullets from the well-oiled gun. She pulled back the lever and pushed away the heavy quilts.

On bare feet, she moved along the wall to the small window by the front door. The moon was high but dim, and all she could see was the outline of a man hunched over. She stepped back when the thunderous knock was accompanied by a plea.

"Anyone in there?"

Emma considered not responding. No lamps were lit, but the remnants of logs burned in the fire. The man would not believe the cabin was empty, and if he did, he might decide to come in anyway.

"Who are you?" Emma quelled her nervousness.

"Thank God. Casey Latimer, ma'am."

Latimer.

Emma slowly lifted the bar blocking the door. She moved a few paces back. "Come on in but be warned. I'm armed."

The door swung open and the man stumbled inside, falling at Emma's feet.

"If it's all the same to you, ma'am, I'll just stay here."

Emma waited, but she only heard the man's heavy and ragged breathing. With one hand holding the Colt, she lit a lamp and returned to stand beside the stranger. Her bare feet stepped in something wet and sticky. She lowered the lamp until it illuminated the small pool of blood seeping between the cracks in the boards and staining the edge of the rug.

"Gracious, Mr. Latimer, what have you done?" Emma set the lamp on her eating table, and after a deep breath and moment's hesitation, she lay the pistol down beside it. "You might have at least fallen inside far enough for me to close the door."

Emma gingerly pulled underneath his arms, but he was too large. She then tried to move his legs enough to secure the door against any animals that might smell the blood and come looking for an easy meal. She spent a few seconds recovering from the exertion of maneuvering the long legs and studied her unexpected guest.

"At least you had the good sense to pass out." Emma hurried to lay the quilts from her bed on the floor. She grit her teeth and raised the edges of her long, white nightgown. Once more, she attempted to drag the unconscious man but to no avail. "I want to apologize in advance, Mr. Latimer." She rolled him once, hefting his body closer to the fire. From there, she managed to lift first his torso, and then his legs, onto the quilts. Long strands of copper hair fell from her loose braid, and she quickly secured the heavy mass before returning to her patient.

"Let's see what you've done to yourself." Emma removed his long coat away from the injured side. The dark shirt beneath was soaked through. "There's no help for it. The shirt must go."

Emma hurried to gather supplies and retrieve the lamp from the table. She cut through his wool shirt and peeled back the edges. A wound, long and deep, scored the side of his chest, curving along the ribs. Her concentration set, Emma soaked up the blood around the injury. Methodically she cleaned the wound and checked for signs of dirt or foreign material. Satisfied that she'd done all she could, Emma threaded one of her needles and stitched the skin until a meticulous line of silk sutures replaced the jagged cut.

Emma sat back on her feet, rolled her shoulders, and then reached for an amber bottle. She spared a quick glance at the patient before pouring a healthy dose of the liquid over the stitches. Latimer twitched and his body shifted, but his eyes remained closed.

Once she'd done all she could, Emma gathered her supplies and cleaned up the blood from the floor. A few more logs were added to the dying fire, and she tossed the bloody rags into the ash. The cloth ignited and the flames returned to life. She draped the last blanket from her bed over the long body.

After she scrubbed her hands in a basin of cold water, she sat in her grandmother's rocker. Her husband had lovingly transported the rocker and her books across the plains and over mountains because a stubborn wife had refused to leave them behind.

The Colt rested in her lap. "You better wake up in the morning, Mr. Latimer because I don't want to have to explain a dead man in my cabin to the sheriff."

EMMA JERKED AWAKE at the sound of riders coming toward the cabin. One look told her that the morning sun had barely kissed the mountain peaks. Her guest still slept. Emma slipped a coat over her nightgown and pulled back the curtain covering the window. Two riders and that was one too many. She could shoot what she aimed at but wouldn't manage more than one before they got her.

"Anybody home?"

The shout came from the taller of the two men. Emma glanced down at Mr. Latimer. "Now would be a good time to wake up." She returned her attention to the men outside, hoping they would simply go away, but the taller one dismounted. Colt in hand and ready, Emma unbarred the door and opened it enough to look out but not enough for the men to see inside.

"What do you want?"

The man's eyes trailed her from bare feet to loose hair, and Emma shuddered.

"Blacksmith in town said the doc lived out here."

She nodded once. "Is someone hurt?"

"No, ma'am. We're looking for a fellow who might have ridden by here. He'll be looking for a doctor."

"Who is the man?"

"That's not your concern, ma'am. Has anyone come by?"

Emma bristled. "I may have helped someone last night. Knife wound."

"Did you fix him up?"

"I'm a doctor. I don't choose who I help."

"Did he say where he was going?"

Emma smiled. "He didn't say much of anything."

The man tipped his hat and stepped forward. Emma raised the Colt. "Keep back. I'm not inviting you inside."

He laughed. "You won't have much choice." The stranger turned and called out to his friend. "Tie up the horses, Jeb."

"The lady said you weren't invited."

Emma stilled as the door opened wider. Her hand dropped to her side, but she managed to keep the Colt steady and pointed toward the stranger.

"Latimer." The man returned his gaze to her. The noise he made sounded to Emma like the growl of a trapped raccoon.

"Stay inside."

Latimer, much like the grizzly bear she witnessed from afar facing down a pack of wolves last winter, faced the two men. Emma ignored his order and pushed past until she stood in front of him. Latimer leaned heavily against the exterior wall while blood seeped through his shirt. Emma held the Colt dead center at the man's chest. "I don't know who you are or why you're here, but you'll leave now or die where you stand."

Emma's bravado didn't impress either man if their laughter was any indication. She felt Latimer's hand on her shoulder. Emma stood her ground and moved until her back pressed firmly against his chest. She heard his heavy breaths and knew he didn't have much time before he collapsed again.

The man on the ground placed one foot forward but paused when Emma pulled the lever back on the pistol. "When I put a bullet in someone, I don't bother taking it out again."

"Come on, Morgan. We'll have another chance." Jeb, who had not dismounted, tossed Morgan his reins.

"You'll be sorry, Doc, and you too, Latimer. This isn't done!" The pair rode away, glancing back every now and then until they were little more than specks of dust on the horizon.

Latimer was growing weaker. Emma turned and circled his waist with her arm. "That was foolish." She helped him struggle inside and managed to take part of his weight and walk him back to the makeshift bed by the fire.

His strong form landed with a gentle thud on the blankets. "I don't suppose you have anything strong and liquid in this cabin."

Emma looked him over, her eyes assessing him. "Strong drink is not what you need right now." She left him alone and instructed him to remove his coat and what was left of his shirt. "I was unable to completely remove your shirt last night, and I need to check for more wounds."

"There aren't any."

"How can you be certain? You appear to be in worse condition than I first thought."

Latimer folded his long duster over twice and set it aside. "The only other wound you'd find is a healed-over hole when I caught a bullet in the shoulder."

Emma wiped her hands dry and carried the bowl of warm water and clean cloths across the small room. She pointed at what remained of his shirt covering the injury. "I'll have to re-stitch that."

Latimer opened his shirt and exposed the wound. Emma knelt down beside him and attempted to work at the awkward angle. She leaned back. "You'll need to lie down."

She didn't appreciate the smirk that flashed across his face, but she ignored it and set to work. Once she was certain the laceration wouldn't open again, she sat back and studied her patient. His body had not twitched once as she re-stitched the wound.

Latimer lowered his eyes and gently pressed his fingers around the clean and precise stitches. "David was right about you. You're a fine doctor." Latimer looked back up at her, and she saw both sincerity and secrets in his eyes. "He was a good man, Mrs. Hawkins."

"Yes, he was." Emma walked to a large trunk at the end of the bed and lifted a heavy black shirt from beneath a pile of her clothes. "You'll need this." She then moved a few of her personal items to the other side of the cabin. Her home boasted only one room, but a small section allowed for privacy when a curtain was strung across. Emma had only closed the area off once when her brother brought David's body back to Crooked Creek. Her brother enlisted for the North after that, and it was the last time she saw him alive.

"And a good friend."

Emma no longer had tears left to shed for a man she barely knew but once loved. "Yes, he was." With the curtain closed, she changed into a clean dress and made hasty work of cleaning her teeth. When she pushed aside the barrier, she saw that Latimer was no longer where she left him. A study of the area outside her window showed her that he'd been a gentleman despite his injuries.

She stepped onto the front steps, a heavy shawl draped over her shoulders. "You shouldn't move around."

"David wouldn't forgive me if I had remained inside." His fingers moved over something hard and metal, grasped in his palm, but Emma could not see what it was. "I was afraid you wouldn't know me. I had nowhere else to go."

Emma stared out over the green pasture below a backdrop of snow-peaked mountains and blue sky dotted with clouds ready to quench the earth. "David sent a letter at the beginning of the war. It told of an old friend he met on the battlefield."

"We went our separate ways after West Point, but when I wrote and told him that I'd volunteered for the sharp shooters, he was hell-bent on joining, too. It was as though the years in between had never happened." Latimer continued to press down on the round object. "I told him not to come. He was safe up here and might have spent those four years running off bandits and natives, but he would still be alive."

Emma smiled and closed her eyes. She could barely see him in her mind, but she remembered everything about him. "It wasn't in him not to go. He came west for me, but his heart and loyalty were still with his family in the East."

"Do you ever miss home?"

Emma shook her head. "When David

first left, and I was here alone, I thought of going back, but my life was here. I wanted no part of that war or the life of despair left behind. The people of Crooked Creek are my family now."

Latimer opened his palm and handed her the object. "He wanted you to have this."

Emma lifted the gold pocket watch from Latimer's hand. Finally, she felt the tears fall. "I gave this to him for luck. My father brought it with him from Scotland." She smiled, wiping the moisture from her cheeks. "David told me a man doesn't find luck. He has to make it." Emma turned her tear-streaked face. "Thank you for bringing it home." She tucked it into her pocket and crossed her arms over her chest. "What will you do now?"

"I didn't share David's love for the city.

This here," Latimer glanced out toward the mountains. "This is the life a man is meant to live." He looked at her now. "Did you set out to settle in Crooked Creek? Life in Montana is a significant change from the comforts of life in the east."

Latimer shifted, but Emma saw the pain it caused him. Instead of answering his question, she said, "You can't ride until you've healed. Let's get you back inside."

"Is there a hotel or boarding house in town?"

Emma nodded. "There's a boarding house, but I have a small room behind my clinic. I sleep there from time to time when a patient needs looking after. It's comfortable and you're welcome to it."

Latimer grinned. "I don't know how much looking after I'll need in a day or so, but I am grateful to you for saving my life."

Emma indicated his wound. "How did you come by that injury, Mr. Latimer, and who were those men?"

"Please, call me Casey. An old argument from the war."

"Only if you'll call me Emma." She watched him struggle to his feet and step a few paces away. "Will they be back?"

"Probably." Latimer looked back out over the land. The horses grazed quietly on early-autumn grass. "They won't hurt you, I promise."

"I don't intend to let them." Emma stood and brushed off her skirts. She studied the land on which she'd made plans and began to build dreams. David's departure had saddened her, but it hadn't shattered her hope—or her determination. Everything she fought for was here. The land was more than she could handle alone, but she refused to relinquish even a small part of her plans and leave any of it behind.

"I'll fix us breakfast, and then while you're resting, I need to get into town." She held the door open, waiting for him to come back inside.

THE TOWN OF Crooked Creek had welcomed David and Emma Hawkins nearly five years ago. Like Emma, the town was built on hope and survived on strength. A war couldn't change that, and though it happened more than two thousand miles away, the war had changed her and everyone else who'd sent loved ones into a battle no one wanted, but knew was necessary.

Emma drove the pair of horses through

town, the sturdy wagon rattling over the ruts formed in the mud by the last heavy rain. She preferred that Latimer remain at the cabin for another day to rest, but he insisted on joining her, and Emma discovered that he was more stubborn than she.

"Sorry about that." Emma pulled on the reins and climbed down from the wagon. Latimer managed to step down, but she saw him wince when his feet hit the ground.

"Dr. Hawkins!"

The young boy's voice had Emma spinning around, one hand on Latimer's strong arm. "Malachi Perkins, why aren't you in school?"

The young boy bent over, attempting to speak while catching his breath. "It's the teacher, ma'am."

Emma lifted her bag from the wagon to

follow the boy, but he shook his head and ran in the other direction.

"We need the sheriff!"

Emma hesitated, then told Latimer to wait for her. She ran down the dirt road to the small building used as a school house. Miss Patterson, the teacher for only three months, lay on the board floor between the center desks. Emma asked the older children to clear the room while she bent over to examine the teacher, still alive. The children didn't move. Emma's eyes drifted up to their frightened faces.

"Doreen," she called out for the oldest girl, but Doreen remained still. Emma's gaze followed the girl's to the man in the shadows by the back door.

Morgan stepped into the light. "I said we'd be back."

Emma lifted herself off the floor, nearly tripping on her skirts. She moved to stand between the children and the man she recognized as Jeb standing by the back door. Emma pushed the remaining children closer to the front of the classroom.

"Don't go and do that, Doc."

She stared into hard dull-blue eyes and cringed at the sight of black teeth showing between a wicked smile. "You don't need them for whatever you have planned. I'll stay, but let them go."

After a brief consideration, Morgan nodded once. Emma didn't hesitate and quickly hurried the children out of the schoolhouse. She remained by the open door until the last child was far enough away. She heard the shouts coming from town and watched as young Malachi, who bravely escaped unnoticed, stood next to the others outside, the aging sheriff beside him, a hand on his pistol.

Strangely, he did not move forward. Emma had treated the sheriff for gout the week before—it was time for him to retire—and hoped someone else came quickly enough to help. Casey Latimer was nowhere to be seen, and she hoped he would stay put considering his condition.

Morgan stepped forward. "Close that door."

The heavy click of a chamber on a pistol forced Emma to comply.

"Now what? The sheriff is out there. You won't get away."

His laughed sickened her, but she managed to keep her expression neutral. "I don't intend to. When that good for nothing didn't die from my knife, I expected him to find the nearest doc, and the fool came here. Doc Hawkins, that is your name, right?"

Emma nodded.

"Wife to that Yankee, David Hawkins."

Emma stiffened, realizing this was much more than settling an old score from the war. "What is it you want?"

"You want me, Morgan."

So much for staying put, Emma thought. She trained her eyes on the open door, the deep and comforting voice giving her a small measure of hope and an equal measure of fear for Latimer's life. The man slowly turned, and Latimer spoke with an almost cavalier attitude. "Jeb won't be coming to help you."

"I didn't hear no gun."

"I didn't fire one." Latimer stepped into the school room and closed the back door. For every step he took forward, Morgan took two back until he was pressed up against the wall.

Emma's focus shifted to Miss Patterson

when the other woman's arm twitched. Mindful of both Latimer and Morgan's positions, Emma crawled a few feet to the teacher and felt for a pulse. Glass from the small window in the room shattered, spraying bits toward her. She covered the teacher's body with her own as best she could and almost feared looking up when a thud and deep-throated scream filled the small space.

Miss Patterson shifted beneath her, but the woman's eyes remained closed. Emma raised herself up and looked around. Morgan lay slumped against the wall, sitting in shards of glass. His hands pressed against his leg while he writhed and shouted at the pain. Never one set to panic, Emma quickly shifted her eyes until they settled on Latimer, barely standing against the door frame.

Emma pushed herself off the ground

and rushed to his side before he collapsed. "I'm grateful you came, truly, but let's see to your wound." The sheriff would take care of Morgan now that the gunfighter was less of a danger, so Emma could once more see to Casey and Miss Patterson—once she got him back to her clinic.

Latimer smiled, but his low laughter turned to a cough. She helped ease him down to rest on the floor.

"Is it as bad as it looks?"

Emma pulled aside his coat to see not only the blood from the wound, but open cuts from the fight with Morgan. "Worse, I imagine."

THREE DAYS HAD passed, and Emma still knew nothing of why the men came searching for Latimer, or why they spoke with such disdain toward her husband. Casey had caught fever. In the daylight hours, he slept almost peacefully, but when darkness came, he thrashed as though demons of the war haunted him. Emma had seen it before in some of her patients but had yet to find a way to relieve these men, and sometimes women, of their nightmares.

It wasn't until Casey's fever broke, and his laceration showed signs of healing, that Emma managed a full night's sleep. She checked on Casey who still slept, and then stepped out onto the front porch of her clinic. The townsfolk went about their business, a few stopping to say hello as they passed by. Emma closed her eyes and soaked in the rays of light from the morning sun.

The clatter of wagon wheels and gentle clip of horses' hooves drew her attention to the small regiment of soldiers riding into town.

When the squad of soldiers stopped in front of her clinic, the officer, a lieutenant of strong bearing and striking features, looked down at her with fierce green eyes. "We're looking for the doctor."

"I'm Doctor Emma Hawkins."

The lieutenant hesitated for a moment. Emma was used to the curious glances and uncertainty from strangers—especially men—who weren't used to women doctors. "We have an injured man in the wagon."

Emma pushed away from the beam and walked swiftly to the wagon. A man lay half-covered with a wool army blanket that had seen a few battles of its own. The lieutenant climbed down from his mount and stood beside her. "We had to cut away some of his clothes, and our men did what they could in the field, but he's caught an infection."

She pulled back a corner of the blanket to reveal a blue, almost black, discoloration on both legs. She felt the skin, clammy and warm beneath her touch.

"Can you help him?"

Emma looked up at the lieutenant. "His gangrene is severe. He might not keep the legs."

"Please, do what you can, Doctor."

Emma nodded and directed the men to carry the soldier inside. She closed the door to the small room where Latimer slept. She washed her hands and cleaned the soldier's legs. A young man of no more than twenty years, he reminded Emma of her younger brother.

"Lieutenant, I need you to stay and help, but your men must wait outside."

Emma mixed together medicinal powders, grinding them with a stone, before setting them in a cup and pouring hot water over them. She gently raised the soldier's head, asking the lieutenant to hold him steady while she slowly poured the drink down the young man's throat. Emma glanced up at the lieutenant. "That should make him a little more comfortable while I tend to him."

The legs were another matter, and after carefully examining them, she did her best to hide her despair. "I cannot save the legs. The infection has likely gone to his bones, and it will continue to spread and probably kill him."

"What are his chances?"

Emma raised and dropped her shoulders. "I don't know. The infection may already have spread too far.

Removing the legs may only quicken his death. I can alleviate some of the pressure and give him medicine for the pain and to help with the infection after the surgery. You'll need to hold him down."

Emma pointed to the wash basin and gathered the instruments and bandages she would need. "How did this happen?"

The lieutenant hesitated, his eyes not wavering from hers. "Two men robbed a bank a week back. Corporal Fenton here was in the contingent who went looking for them. I only just arrived from Washington and found him like this at camp."

Emma shifted uncomfortably. "Who were the men?"

"Morgan and Jeb Allen. Brothers who have been robbing and killing since they deserted about a month before the war ended."

"Southerners?"

"Yes, ma'am, and we've been charged now with bringing them in, dead or alive, for their crimes during and after the war."

The door creaked behind Emma, and she noticed the new direction of the officer's eyes.

"You'll have to take one of them dead. Morgan is over at the sheriff's. The Doc here patched him up, so he's all yours."

Can the man not follow simple instructions and stay in bed? Emma wondered. "Mr. Latimer, if you're pulling your stitches again, you'll end up back on this table where this poor young soldier is right now."

The officer started in surprise. "Casey Latimer?"

Latimer nodded and stepped up to the

foot of the table. Blood seeped from the thin cuts Emma made in the boy's legs.

"My commander told me to warn you that the Allens were headed your way."

"They found me."

Emma wrapped the wounds with white cloths, the stark contrast between blood and bandage a painful reminder of her husband's battered body ravaged by war.

"Lieutenant, the pressure should be more bearable and I'll give him morphine for the pain."

"How long?"

Aware of what he was asking her, Emma said, "A few days, perhaps a few weeks. He can remain here."

"Appreciate that, ma'am, but I know the boy's family, and I prefer to take him home. It's only a few days' journey—can he make it?"

Cautious, Emma could not make any

guarantees. "If he survives the night, then he'll have a chance to make it home."

"Thank you, ma'. . . Doctor Hawkins." The lieutenant tipped his hat. "My men will be by to collect him in the morning."

Emma watched the officer leave and lowered herself to the bench against the wall. The procedure had taken her a little more than hour. She tended to lose time while she operated.

Latimer lowered himself down to the unoccupied portion of the bench.

"You look better today."

"Thought you might lose me?"

Emma leaned her head back and closed her eyes for a few seconds. "I knew the first night in my cabin that you would survive. Were it not for stubborn foolishness, you might have healed sooner." She settled her back against the wall. "I didn't have a chance to thank you for saving me and Miss Patterson over at the school. Thank you."

He nodded absently. "Is the teacher all right?"

"Yes, just a few bruises from the fall and a painful cut where she was hit on the head, but nothing serious." Emma sat forward, her eyes watching the young soldier's chest rise and fall with each shallow breath. "I've had enough of not knowing. I must insist you tell me why the Allen brothers came after you."

"It's not a pleasant story."

She stared at him with resolve until he stood and walked to the table, his gaze dropping to the battered body of the young soldier. "It was after the battle at Fort Henry."

Emma stiffened. It was a short time after that when David was returned to her.

"The skirmish was small but fatal. David and I were with a small group of scouts when we came upon our targets. We split up, but one of the smugglers— they had proven to be more ruthless than the worst of the Southern soldiers— found David and killed him, though not before he took down a few of them. I didn't get there in time because I was on the other side blowing up the barn and wagons they used to store munitions. Two of the Allen brothers died that day and two got away."

"You would have killed them that day at the cabin."

"I would have tried." Latimer grinned. "But a stubborn spitfire had other plans."

Emma's smile was slow to form, but when she did, it felt good. She returned to the table where the soldier's breathing came easier. "You must have seen this before on the battlefields. I've treated a few cases of gangrene, but nothing this severe."

Latimer nodded. "I wish we had more doctors in the field, then maybe a lot of young men might have made it home, even if only to say good-bye."

THE NEXT MORNING, Emma watched the lieutenant and his soldiers drive away with young Fenton in the back of the army wagon, prepared as comfortably as they could manage for the long journey. The boy was strong and had a good chance of making it home before he passed. Latimer stood beside her, his presence a new and welcome part of her life. Some of the townsfolk also stopped and watched as the wagon rolled out of

Crooked Creek.

"This is a nice town you and David found."

"It's certainly a sharp contrast from life out east, but it's home and I'm content here." Emma watched a few children playing in the tall grass near the school. Classes wouldn't resume fully until Miss Patterson mended, but Doreen offered to teach a few lessons each day. Emma turned to Latimer. "Will you walk with me? I have something to show you."

Latimer stepped off the boardwalk and held out his arm. Careful not to brush up against his bandage, Emma looped her arm through his and settled her palm on his arm. They walked past the school and church and to the top of a hill overlooking the town. She released her arm and knelt down in front of a simple headstone.

"He would have wanted to say goodbye."

Latimer joined her on the ground and pulled a knife from the belt of his pants. "I've been carrying this with me ever since the night David died."

Emma stiffened. "That's what killed him?"

Latimer nodded. He dug beneath the grass down to the dirt and set the knife into the earth, covering it over. "I am sorry he's the one who didn't come home to you." His hand rested against the grave.

Emma reached out and covered Latimer's hand. "David lived a good life, and he wouldn't wish your death just so he could be here."

"He talked of the plans he'd made with you—often."

"David was a wonderful man, and he would have stayed in Montana for me, but it's not where he wanted to be. I knew that in my heart. If the war hadn't killed him, this wilderness might have." She pulled her hand back. Latimer stood and helped her up, but kept her fingers locked with his.

Emma turned and watched the town below, guarded by the mountains on three sides, and a river so blue and wild that she wondered how anyone could live anywhere else. She leaned back to look up at him. "Where will you go from here?"

"Crooked Creek looks like a good place to begin again."

Looking at Emma, Latimer draped his arm over Emma's shoulders and guided her back down the hill. The setting sun kissed the peaks of the craggy mountains and a pair of eagles soared overhead toward the sunset. She had no idea what awaited her tomorrow, but Emma knew she had a purpose, and a life she loved, in Crooked Creek.

THE END

Thank you for reading "Emma of Crooked Creek"!

Scroll through to enjoy "Hattie of Crooked Creek," the next story in the Crooked Creek series.

HATTIE OF CROOKED CREEK

MK MCCLINTOCK

She proved she was strong enough to survive.
He proved he was strong enough to love her.

Married three months before the war and now a widow, Harriett McBride can either give up and sell her ranch or fight for the life she and her husband came west to build. With the help of a friend and a stranger, she must stop the one who threatens all she holds dear. When Hattie is faced with an unexpected choice, will she bury her heart on the battlefield forever or find a way to love again?

HATTIE OF CROOKED CREEK

Crooked Creek, Montana Territory
October 1865

HATTIE STARED UP at the early morning rays as they glistened through her watery grave. She should have known better than to ride out before the sun rose above the craggy peaks, but she had to prove herself day after day, if to no one else but herself.

Glen Meek, her foreman, scolded her two mornings ago when he learned that she'd been heading out on her own in the mornings before he and young John, his nephew, had even put their heads on the pillow from the night before.

Hattie had waved off Glen's concern with a distracting grin and a load of grit. The McBride Ranch was Hattie's responsibility, her late husband's legacy, and no one would take it away from her.

Lights swam through the sky above her. If she reached out far enough, her fingers might be able to skim the surface of a star before the sun's light washed them all away. She must have fallen into the river. Her shift clung to her body as though wet, but she knew how to swim. Why, then, did the black waters of unconsciousness seem determined to carry her away?

The raging fire burned within as her lungs expanded. The pounding on her chest surely couldn't be good for her ribs.

"Don't do this. Stay with me."

Her lungs exhaled, but instead of air, water escaped from her mouth in a frenzy of coughs.

"That's right, let it all out."

Twigs and small rocks dug into her back, but she lay flat and ignored them. Sunlight threatened her eyes to open.

"You're going to make it."

What was he talking about? The words didn't make it past her thoughts. Her lips still scorched from the heat, of what she didn't know. Her body no longer lay upon the hard earth, and her mind began to wake to a greater awareness.

"Put me down."

Of course, the man couldn't hear her. She barely heard the scratchy whisper.

"I said—"

"I heard you, Mrs. McBride, but I'm not putting you down."

Hattie's arm disobeyed her when she tried to reach for the colt strapped to her hip. Her captor, though apparently strong, handled her with great care, but Hattie knew the worst of what could happen to her awaited. "So this must be Hell."

HATTIE AWAKENED TO a soft humming and the gentle creak of a rocking chair swaying to and fro on a wooden floor. Warmth surrounded her body, and the twigs and rocks of the hard earth had been replaced by downy comfort.

"It's about time you came back to us."

Hattie tilted her head when the woman sat on the edge of the bed. "Emma?"

"At least your mind isn't addled." Emma pressed the cold end of her stethoscope to Hattie's chest. "We almost lost you. Carson has paced a hole in my waiting room floor."

Hattie's eyes closed once more as a rush

of memories overwhelmed her. A strong and determined face hovered above her own. Eyes, blue as her clear mountain lake, pressed through the memories.

"Carson?" Hattie started to rise. "By all that's holy." The piercing pain forced her back against the pillows.

"Stay put or you'll ruin all my hard work." Emma poured a glass of water, and though Hattie didn't like the idea of someone helping her drink, the cool liquid eased the burning in her throat.

Hattie's mind might be a little rattled, but the events that led her to the clinic bed began to return. She watched Emma mix a white powder into another glass of water. "What's that?"

"It will help with the pain."

"Blazes to the pain." Hattie's wound chose that moment to mock her. "Will it put me out?"

Emma smiled and held out the glass as though Hattie didn't have much a choice. "It will help keep your fever down. Your temperature spiked yesterday, and I'm not about to let that happen again."

Hattie downed the foul liquid and handed the glass back to Emma. "Who's Carson?"

"You don't know him?" Emma asked with a look of combined surprise and concern.

Hattie shook her head and tried to readjust her arm. "Is he the one who brought me in?"

Emma nodded. "Carson White Eagle. He keeps to himself mostly. I patched him up in the spring after he had a run-in with a mountain lion."

Hattie watched as Emma tidied up the large wooden tray covered in bandages and small instruments. "Please send him up, Emma. I'd like to thank him."

Emma paused at the doorway, the tray balanced expertly on one hand. "Do you remember what happened out there?"

The ache in Hattie's side confirmed that she'd been shot, but by who or what remained in the dark recesses of her mind. "I will, I'm sure. Has this Mr. White Eagle said anything about when he found me?"

"Sheriff Epps spoke to him, but I was too busy keeping you alive to find out what Carson told him. Glen and John are crazy with worry. John heard the gunshots but didn't think they were close enough to be a concern. He's blaming himself for not checking on the situation."

Hattie silently cursed but couldn't ignore the guilt. It wasn't the first time she'd gone out on her own in the early mornings, and it wouldn't be the last. "It's not his fault."

"Carson told him as much. I sent Glen and John back to the ranch with the promise that we'd send word when you woke up."

"I'll tell them myself when I get home." Hattie tugged at the quilt covering most of her body. "Emma?"

The doctor turned in the open doorway.

"Thank you."

Emma left to find Carson, and Hattie closed her eyes to rest for a minute.

HATTIE MUST HAVE drifted to sleep for when she next opened her eyes, her body protested even the slightest movement. She stared up at the ceiling instead.

"You're all right."

Hattie fought the urge to moan when

she shifted her weight in order to sit up. A stranger's face, attached to a broad-shouldered man, came into focus. He possessed dark hair the color of coal buried deep in the mountains and eyes bluer than a Montana sky on a late summer day. A healed scar, barely visible through his dark stubble, marred the corner of his upper lip.

"I'll live, and it seems I have you to thank for that. How long have you been standing there?"

"A while. Anyone would have done it, ma'am," Carson was quick to add.

"It's Hattie, but you already know my name." Hattie managed to prop one of the pillows behind her lower back, but it wasn't without difficulty. Carson crossed the room to her side and added another pillow to the pile. "Thank you."

Carson nodded. "I do know your name,

Mrs. McBride."

"You have an advantage over me, Mr. White Eagle." Hattie studied the way Carson's jaw tightened when she said his full name.

"Everyone around here knows who you are Mrs. McBride. A woman making a go of it on a horse ranch in the Montana mountains is bound to be noticed. Unusual, and not too smart."

Hattie bristled under the unexpected insult. "I manage just fine, and I'm not alone out there."

"An old man and a young boy are hardly—"

"Just how much do you know about me, Mr. White Eagle?"

Carson stalled, but for what reason Hattie couldn't fathom. After a long pause, he said, "I live in the mountains above your ranch."

Hattie knew someone lived on the mountain, of course. It was land her husband had tried to purchase without success up until the time he enlisted. Hattie hadn't bothered to pursue the purchase because the two thousand acres she already owned proved to be more than enough for her horses and cattle. What she had heard didn't correspond with the man standing before her now. Some had claimed he was an Indian warrior who left his band, others had claimed he was a scar-faced half-breed whose only friends were the wild mustangs that roamed the hills and valleys.

Other than his name, nothing indicated Carson White Eagle wasn't as white-born as Hattie. His manners, as she recalled, might have started out poorly, but under the circumstances, hers were deplorable.

With regret heavy in her voice, Hattie said, "I'm sorry, Mr. White Eagle. You saved my life and for that I am truly grateful."

"I'm not 'Mr.' anything, Mrs. McBride, just Carson. I'm only sorry I didn't reach you sooner."

Hattie recalled leaving her cabin that morning and setting off to the high pastures. She enjoyed the first hour before sunrise when the herd and her horse kept her company while she savored nature's music. She especially loved the crisp mornings of autumn when the rustling of fallen leaves joined the chorus of waterfowl and warblers making their way south for the winter. The narrow river which crisscrossed its way over her land from the mountain peaks rushed over tumbled rocks, offering a perfect backdrop to the early birds' melody.

That morning, the loud report of a gun blast echoing off the mountains had interrupted the beautiful symphony.

"Would you mind telling me what you did see and hear?"

"You don't remember?"

Hattie shook her head, and Carson lowered himself back into the chair Emma had occupied a short while ago.

"I remember the gunshot, and then the river pulled me under. I saw your face, felt myself lifted up, and then the next thing I remember is I waking up here."

Carson sat on the edge of the chair as though prepared to jump up and bolt. "I was about a mile away, tending to one of the mustangs when I heard the shot. When I got there, you'd fallen in the river."

"Did you see anyone else?"

Carson nodded. "I fired at him, but it was either save you or catch him. Easier to search for the man later than bring you back from the dead."

Hattie chuckled. "I don't believe I've heard it put so well. I thank you again for saving my life."

Carson looked ready to leave, but Hattie's quiet words stopped him and surprised her. "Would you mind sitting with me until Emma returns?"

He didn't hesitate and settled against the back of the large rocker. Hattie asked, "How is it you've never come down to the ranch in all these years?"

"Most folks don't take kindly to people like me. I'd just as soon keep to myself."

"People like you? I'm not sure I understand."

Carson tensed, the subtle change not lost on Hattie. "That's because you're not from around here, Mrs. McBride." He stood then, intent on a quick exit. "I'll tell Emma you're awake."

Without a backward glance or fare-thee-well, Carson existed the room, his boots on the floorboards surprisingly silent.

Hattie looked at the doorway where only a moment before, her guardian angel had stood. The image of his chiseled features were seared into her thoughts. His words, "people like me," told her that she wasn't the only one who had heard the stories of the half-breed who played with the mustangs and rarely ventured down to the valley. Hattie woke up every morning, stood on her front porch, and stared up at that mountain, knowing that it stood as both a guardian and a threat to her ranch. She'd ventured halfway up once with her husband, but a rock slide had forced them back down. She decided the mountain was better off left alone, as were its inhabitants.

"You don't look much better." Emma walked into the room carrying another tray, this time burdened with a small bowl and covered serving dish. "You need to eat something."

"I am famished." Hattie closed her eyes and inhaled the spicy aroma. "Is that mushroom soup?"

Emma nodded. "Bess is serving it to her guests for lunch at the boarding house. She's been by twice, and a few others from town have stopped in asking about you." Emma ladled the fragrant soup in the smaller bowl and handed the dish with a spoon to Hattie. "Eat every drop, and when you're done, I need you to rest."

"I've rested." Hattie enjoyed the first

spoonful. "I'd get fat if I ate Bess's cooking every day, but a wide girth would be worth it." She quickly devoured the remaining soup.

"More?"

Hattie grinned and handed back the bowl. "I'd better not. Did Mr. White Eagle leave?"

"He doesn't like to be called 'Mr.'"

"So he told me." Hattie couldn't shake the image of the tall, blue-eyed man who had rescued her, and she wanted to learn more about him. "Did Mr. . . . Carson say where he was going?"

Emma chuckled. "Carson doesn't tell anyone much of anything."

"I need to know what else he might have seen. Someone shot me, Emma, and he saw the person."

Emma's smile vanished. "Carson breathed life back into you, and I pulled that bullet from your chest. We didn't save your life just so you could chase the bastard who tried to take it away." Emma huffed and calmed down. "And I won't apologize for my language. Lord, you're stubborn."

Hattie reached out and gently gripped Emma's arm. "I can't repay what you and Carson have done, but I will find out who shot me and why."

"You need to be careful, Hattie. The man missed, and he's still out there. Leave it to the sheriff."

Hattie released her grip on Emma's arm. "When Casey Latimer showed up on your doorstep half-dead and bleeding, you fixed him up. When those men came to your door looking for him, you held a gun on them and would have killed them both, if necessary."

"I was defending my patient and my

home. It's not the same."

"Yes, it is. Whoever pulled that trigger did it on my land." Hattie watched a variety of emotions play over her friend's face before it settled on concern.

"Truth be told, Carson is probably out looking for the man right now."

"What?" Hattie flung the blankets off her body and forced her legs over the edge of the bed.

"Get back in bed."

Hattie ignored Emma and pushed her body up, ignoring the excruciating pain in her side. "I'm going home."

"You'll bleed out before you get there."

"I've seen your work. The stitches will hold so long as I don't ride. I'll rent a wagon if I have to, but I'm going home." Hattie struggled to the edge of the bed and fell against the footboard.

"Obstinate is too nice of a word for you

right now. Glen is waiting outside with your wagon, but you won't need it yet." Emma propped Hattie up with her own body weight.

"What the hell do you think you're doing?"

Hattie struggled to raise her head. Carson rushed to her side and took over where Emma had labored under Hattie's taller frame. Instead of bracing her, Carson lifted Hattie and set her back in the bed.

"I need to get home."

"You can barely stand."

Carson rubbed a hand over the stubble on his jaw and glared at Hattie with ice-blue eyes. If Hattie was a betting woman, which she wasn't, she'd say that more often than not, people underestimated Carson White Eagle.

"I can't stay in bed while the—"

"He's gone."

Hattie looked up at Carson. "What do you mean, gone? I can track him, I know I can." Hattie once more pulled back the covers, but Carson stopped her. Emma gave Hattie a sly smile and a shrug before walking from the room with the food tray.

"Don't get so riled, Mrs. McBride." Instead of settling in the chair, Carson lowered himself to the edge of the bed. "I followed the tracks about two miles south of where you fell."

Hattie narrowed her eyes. "Which direction?"

"East."

"East is the Yellowstone and beyond the river are wild animals and trappers." Hattie cradled her arm close to her wound, remembering the pain of the bullet and the inability to breathe as her lungs filled with water. "You're certain he went east?"

Carson nodded. "If he crossed the Yellowstone, he could be anywhere by now."

"That's more than thirty miles from where he shot me. Is it possible he was just a horse thief or rustler passing through?"

"It's possible," Carson conceded, but Hattie harbored her own doubts.

"You don't believe that, do you?"

"No, I don't." Carson reached for the pitcher of water on the small table by the bed and filled the glass. He handed it to Hattie, and she automatically took it. "If he had come from the north and happened upon your ranch, then I might believe it was opportunity, but there are easier trails and roads that lead to Crooked Creek."

Hattie drank half the glass of water and considered the man beside her. "Then he came for me, but why?"

"I'll go back to your ranch tomorrow and see if I can pick up a new trail. Could be he rode toward the Yellowstone and then double backed."

Hattie set the now empty glass on the table. "That land is my life, and I should be the one protecting it."

"You don't get it. It's not the land I'm trying to protect." Carson rose and walked to the door. With his hand on the doorframe, he turned around. "It means that much to you?"

Hattie sat forward as much as her sore body would allow. Their eyes met and held, but his revealed nothing. She didn't need his permission to hunt down the man who shot her, just as she didn't need Emma's permission to leave the clinic, but Hattie's parents didn't raise a fool. The hole in her shoulder and residual burning in her lungs told her that she couldn't do this alone.

"Yes."

Carson nodded once. "Rest today. I'll be back in the morning."

HATTIE WALKED FROM one end of the small room to the next. She had discarded the sling an hour ago, moving her arm in every direction she could, testing for range. Needle-like pain turned into a deep throbbing, which she ignored. When Emma entered the room with a breakfast tray, she found Hattie stretching her wounded shoulder, sling abandoned. Emma nearly dropped the tray.

"I swear all sense left you when that bullet hit. What on earth are you doing?"

"It's time for me to get home."

Emma set the tray down and pointed to the bed. "You're not ready."

"I'm as ready as I need to be. Except, my clothes seem to be missing."

Emma's sigh was one of surrender. Hattie might have appreciated Emma's acquiescence if guilt hadn't managed to creep into her conscious. She wouldn't apologize for her decision to leave, regardless of the potential consequences.

"Your clothes were burned; too much blood." Emma left the room and returned a few minutes later with a green calico dress. "Wear this. Your coat has a little blood on it, but I didn't think you'd appreciate me burning that, too."

"Thank you. I mean it. You saved my life, and I'm beholden to you." Hattie smoothed her hand over the green fabric. "This is just something I have to do."

Emma nodded and pointed to the tray. "At least eat something before you leave. Please."

"I will."

"Casey arrived back in town last night, and I told him what happened."

Hattie stilled. "And?"

"He's probably out at your ranch by now."

Hattie rarely had cause to curse, believing it to be language for the most lowly and uneducated of people, but she couldn't always control her thoughts. Right now, those thoughts crossed over from ladylike to provincial. "Wonderful. Now I have two men out there who are going to tell me what to do."

Emma crossed the room and settled her hands on Hattie's good shoulder. "You're not being sensible."

"I know." Hattie's mouth twisted into a

frown. "I'm just stir-crazy, bound up inside."

"All right, then." Emma dropped her hands and headed for the door. "Carson is downstairs waiting for you when you're ready."

"You could have told me that sooner," Hattie called out to Emma, but the doctor had already left the room.

Hattie struggled through a quick washing and the changing into the green calico dress. As promised, she ate most of the breakfast Emma had brought upstairs. Ready, she went downstairs, leaving behind the sling.

Carson leaned against one of the posts holding up the roof of Emma's clinic, staring out at the street. Hattie watched through the window of the clinic door as someone drew his attention. Carson's head barely turned, but Hattie noticed the quick tightening of his shoulders and the almost imperceptible way his hand inched closer to his sidearm.

Crooked Creek had been a somewhat peaceful town since Hattie's arrival, mostly untouched from the war that divided a nation. Even most of the Army-Indian skirmishes were mild compared to what took place in other towns and territories. Had it not been for men going off to fight for either the North or South—and families losing their husbands, fathers, and sons—the town might have gone unscathed. Then the war ended. Those men lucky enough to return home, did so to find families gone and land left wasted. Strangers began to appear in Crooked Creek, and not just the kind passing through, but those looking for a quick and easy opportunity. The familiar lines of the stranger's face piqued

Hattie's interest and prompted her to step outside.

She stood just to Carson's left. "Do you know him?"

Carson readjusted his stance until he faced her rather than the street. "No." He watched as her eyes narrowed in study of the man. "Do you?"

"He's familiar."

"Could be the man who shot you."

Hattie shook her head. "No, it can't, but I've seen him somewhere. Have you met Casey Latimer?"

Carson nodded, the edges of his mouth tilting upward. "Met him this morning. He's at your ranch now."

"Did he find anything?"

"Not before I left." Carson stepped off the clinic porch and held out a hand. Hattie glanced from the hand to the wagon hitched behind Carson and reluctantly accepted his help. It galled her that she had to ride out of town on a wagon rather than her horse, but Carson assured her that one of her men—he thought it was John—had taken care of her mare after the shooting.

Once Hattie settled on the buckboard seat with Carson next to her and his horse tied up to the back, Carson set the pair of Morgan horses in motion with a gentle flick of the reins. Hattie and her husband had brought the Morgans with them from Vermont with plans to breed their own stock. Their plan faltered when Samuel McBride joined the North in the war. Hattie had turned her attention to the horses and cattle because that was the only way to keep her ranch afloat. Three painstaking years into the war, Hattie had managed to pay off their ranch by selling her cattle with some of the larger outfits' stock. Although raising and breeding horses had remained her primary goal, the cattle operation had steadily grown.

"You still with me?"

Hattie shook herself from the reverie and looked at Carson and then at the road ahead. They were now only a mile from her ranch. "I can understand why Casey would help me; he's Emma's fiancé and she's my closest friend, but why are you so invested in my safety? You must have obligations of your own."

Carson stared straight ahead, though Hattie caught a glimpse of a slight grin. "I'd hate to see you killed after I went to so much trouble saving you."

Hattie waited for more, but further explanation wasn't forthcoming. "While I'm sincerely grateful for your concern. Once we get to the ranch, you can return to your mountain. I'll be fine, Mr. White Eagle."

"That's a kind offer, Mrs. McBride, but I'll stick around a while longer." Carson guided the horses and wagon to the front of her ranch house and helped her down, careful to avoid touching her wounded shoulder.

Carson immediately pushed her behind him.

"I'm not a sack of grain Mr.—"

"Quiet."

Hattie stood on her toes to see over Carson's shoulder but saw nothing. He visibly relaxed and stepped to the side. It was then Hattie heard a horse galloping toward them. The familiar rider slowed his black gelding as he approached the house.

Casey touched the tip of his hat and dismounted. "Hattie."

"Emma shouldn't have bothered you with this."

"It's not a bother, you know that."

Hattie didn't miss the quick exchange of grim looks Casey and Carson passed one another. "Both of you listen here and now. I won't have you thinking I can be set aside while you fight my battles for me. I'm grateful that you're both here, truly I am, but neither of you was shot. Whatever is going on, I can't be responsible for harm befalling anyone else."

"Hattie." Carson said only her name in a smooth and tender voice. The one word managed to calm her temper long enough to recognize her bad manners.

Casey remounted and offered Hattie the kind of smile a brother would give his sister. She hadn't known Casey long, but he and Emma were the closest people to family she'd had since her husband left.

"I'm sorry, to both of you."

Casey's initial response was a wide grin. "Don't you worry. If it had been Emma with a bullet in her shoulder, she'd be a lot more ornery than you."

Hattie returned the smile. Casey exchanged one more of those mysterious glances with Carson and then rode off in the direction of town.

"Well, one of you is easier to deal with than two. What did he not want to say in front of me?"

Instead of answering, Carson asked a question of his own. "Are Glen and John the only two you have working here?"

"Amelia Porter from town comes in to help around the house, but she's in Denver with her sister waiting on a new niece or nephew." Hattie stepped closer to Carson, whose eyes had remained fixed on hers. "Why?"

"I'd expected them to be around when you returned home. I saw them just this morning."

A minuscule thread of alarm sneaked its way into Hattie's thoughts, but she quickly pushed it back. "They're likely out with the cattle. After what happened . . . oh, God. If something has happened to either of them—"

"Let's not worry until there's cause for it." Carson stepped down from the porch and untied his horse. "They're likely out with the herd, just as you said." He swung up on the back of his horse, a coal-colored animal splayed with white spots over his hindquarters and neck. "I'll be back soon." Carson and his gelding turned in one fluid movement, rider and animal as one.

Hattie watched him ride toward the

pastures and then through part of the herd. The cattle and horses didn't venture as far as the Yellowstone, but a small stream snaked down from the mountain providing year-round water for her stock. They'd brought the herd in closer when it looked like the weather was going to change for the worse. However, the expected snow held back, allowing the animals more time to graze on the autumn grass. There were always strays to round up and fences to check, two tasks that could take Glen and John to various corners of her vast ranch. Hattie prayed it was the work that kept them away.

After a short time of staring off in the direction Carson rode, Hattie entered the quiet ranch house. She stood in the small foyer and looked around at the home her husband had built for them. Hattie had pounded three of the nails in the first floorboard, her way of contributing to their new way of life. It wasn't the first time she had wielded a hammer nor had it been the last.

Hattie hurried to her bedroom at the back of the house and traded her borrowed clothes from Emma for a riding skirt, button-down shirt, and wool vest. Sore, yet resolved, she marched back to the small, open room adjacent to the front door. Within seconds, she had donned her long canvas riding duster, labored into her favorite pair of riding boots, and reached for the wide-brimmed hat she had bought when she first arrived in Crooked Creek.

It wasn't until she picked up her rifle that her wounded shoulder protested. Ignoring the pain, Hattie made her way to the barn in long, hurried strides. It took her three tries—and a few words she wouldn't repeat in the company of others—to lift her saddle onto the back of her mare.

"Are you looking to get yourself killed?"

Hattie's foot slipped from the stirrup a second time. Her jaw clenched. "No."

Carson swung his leg over the front of his gelding and slid down. "You have a fool way of proving that." He removed her hand from the saddle horn and before she realized what he planned, Carson lifted her onto the mare. His arm swept out in front of him to the barn door. "No one's stopping you."

Hattie's shoulder throbbed, and not with the kind of pain that would eventually go away. "You're angry."

Carson's look proved as much; she didn't need to state the obvious.

"I didn't know how long you'd be, and

they're my men, my responsibility."

Carson stepped forward and looked up at her. At over six feet tall, he didn't have far to look. "And who's responsible for you? Glen and John are back."

"They came in with you? You weren't gone—"

"They were headed back before I rode out too far." Carson quickly added, "They're alive."

"Well, I should hope so." Hattie stepped back from her horse and rushed to the entrance of the stable just as John entered. A litter had been fashioned and attached to John's horse and on that litter lay his father, Glen. John and Carson stood beside the litter where Hattie now knelt beside Glen. "What happened?"

"He caught a bullet ricochet off a rock," John said.

Hattie poked around at the wound that Glen attempted to shrug off. "Accident or intentional?"

"Can't rightly say, Hattie." John lifted his hat and swiped the sweat from his brow. Despite the cool weather, sweat covered both men. John continued, "It was awful close, but he'll be all right. I'll go for the doc once he's settled."

Hattie turned at the touch of Carson's hand on her shoulder. She rose and moved aside so that Carson and John could help Glen up.

"Wait. He should go up to the house."

"I can't do that, Hattie."

"Yes, you can, Glen." Hattie looked at John. "Please take your father up to the house and help him into the spare bedroom upstairs."

John ignored his father's protests and followed Hattie's orders. He maneuvered the horse and litter back outside and followed the well-worn path to the house. Once more alone, Hattie faced Carson.

"Do you know what happened out there?"

As had become his habit, Carson ignored her question and posed one of his own. "Who would want to harm you or your men?"

Hattie walked to the stable door and looked out over her land. Mist had settled low, winding through the pines. An eagle flew over the barn and disappeared over Carson's mountain. "I have absolutely no idea. I keep to myself, work the land and horses. I know most of the townspeople, but don't see them too often."

Carson stepped around Hattie and removed the saddle from her mare's back. Hattie rolled her shoulder and ignored the pain.

"Perhaps Jade Buckman."

Carson guided her horse into a stall and hung the bridle on its hook. He moved around the stable as though he was well acquainted with the building. "Buckman Cattle Company?"

"That's him. He approached Samuel not long after we arrived in Crooked Creek. Buckman had just started buying up land, but Samuel bought our land before we arrived. Samuel turned down his offers. After word spread that Samuel died a few months before the war ended, Buckman approached me again."

"You turned him down."

"Of course. He told me I'd regret it, but I didn't take the threat seriously. I thought he meant that I'd regret the hardship of running this place alone as a woman."

"And he hasn't approached you again

since?"

"No, after Samuel's death was the last time."

The open stable doors rattled when a gust of wind swept through the building. John seemed to blow in with the wind.

"It's turning bad out there." John hurried his horse inside.

"How's your father?"

"He'll be all right. I don't think he'll need Doc Hawkins after all, which would suit Pa just fine."

"I'll ask Emma to come out for a visit just the same. I'd feel better knowing that the wound is properly dressed." Hattie watched Carson watching John, and wondered about Carson's interest in the young man. "You should stay with your father tonight."

John faced her, his arms full of the saddle from his horse. "I hoped you might say that. Thank you. I don't reckon Pa can do much for himself right now."

"I can look after your father regardless of this nuisance injury. He'd feel better if you were close."

John's smiled slightly. "Pa would feel better knowing I was working, Miss Hattie." He finished removing the tack from his horse and secured the animal in the stall next to the mare.

"The day is late and the animals are where they should be. We'll gather the remaining cattle strays tomorrow."

John opened his mouth as if to argue, but then clamped it shut. He thanked Hattie again and rushed from the stable. She watched the young man sprint back to the house where she hoped Glen proved to be a better patient for John than she'd been for Emma.

"I'll go out with John tomorrow."

At some point during her conversation with John, Carson had moved forward without stirring the straw on the ground or scraping his boots on the wooden boards.

"How do you move like that?"

Carson shrugged. "You can't ride."

"You have a bad habit of telling me what to do, Mr. White Eagle."

"And you have a bad habit of calling me 'Mr.' when you're annoyed with me."

Hattie suppressed a smile, but her lips still twitched at the corners. It only took her a few seconds to sober and remember why Carson thought he could tell her what to do. Someone had shot her—almost killed her—and it was likely that the same someone shot at Glen and John.

"This isn't your fight, Carson."

"I suppose we'll have to disagree on that."

In a move that surprised Hattie, Carson gently gripped her arm and guided her from the stable. He secured the doors and turned to face the wind, and to Hattie's keen eye, he appeared to enjoy the thrash of moisture that fell from the sky. Carson returned his hand to her arm and hurried alongside her to the front porch of the house. He released her arm with a slow brush of his fingers and shook the rain from his duster.

Hattie decided that trying to decipher Carson's intentions would only cause her head to ache, and at the moment, her shoulder ached plenty for the rest of her.

"It won't take long to prepare dinner if you'd like to join us."

Carson looked pointedly at her arm, but said nothing about her using it. "I appreciate the offer, but I have somewhere to be. I'll be back tomorrow."

"Where are you off to?"

Carson studied her face, and under his close scrutiny, she foolishly wondered if he liked what he saw.

"Do yourself a favor and don't go anywhere until I return."

"Your bad habit is becoming worse, Mr. White Eagle."

Carson grinned. "So is yours, Mrs. McBride."

TRUE TO HIS word, Carson returned the following afternoon, though Hattie hadn't been alone in the almost twenty-four hours since Carson rode out in the storm. Emma and Casey arrived unexpectedly with provisions. Emma promptly set to work on Glen's wound and soon assured Hattie that her foreman and friend would mend in a few days. Hattie asked what she could do for Glen, and Emma told her she could rest. Casey and John saw to a few chores once the rain abated, and Hattie took the opportunity to shrug back into her coat and boots to look in on the stock. Emma caught her at the door and put herself between Hattie and the exit.

Hattie had had enough.

"Carson might have told you I needed a nursemaid and white knight to look after me, but I've managed well enough for over three years without someone dictating to me."

Emma's unapologetic grin might have irritated Hattie more had she not sounded like a petulant child.

"I'm sorry, Emma. Poor manners seem to be a bad habit of mine lately." Hattie removed her coat and set it over the hook, along with her hat. The boots she left on. "He did tell you to come out and check on me, didn't he?"

"If by 'he' you mean Carson, then no. Although, he did come by early this morning."

Emma held up a finger and shook her head, then headed toward the back of the house to the kitchen. Flames danced in the stone fireplace and steam rose from an iron kettle on the cook stove. Emma motioned for Hattie to sit at the table while her friend prepared tea. Amused that she no longer seemed in control in her own home, Hattie sat.

Emma poured hot water from the kettle into the cup and set it down in front of Hattie. "Carson did tell us Glen had been injured and that you wanted me to examine him. Was he wrong?"

Hattie stared at the golden liquid forming in her cup. She removed the tea infuser and set it aside. "No." She looked up at her friend. "That's all he said?"

"I do recall him saying hello."

Hattie gave up on interrogating Emma and simply enjoyed her friend's company. Emma and Casey insisted on staying the night. Hattie got the impression that an objection would have been ignored.

The following morning, Emma had breakfast fixed before Hattie awakened much later than usual. Casey and John had completed the morning chores, and Glen assured her that he was well enough to join them for breakfast and return to his own cabin.

Hattie felt like a guest in her own home with well-meaning friends all around.

The morning drifted into the early afternoon. Casey and Emma left and John walked with his father to their cabin. As much as she wished for solitude when the house had been full, now Hattie regretted the silence. She wasn't able to ride her land, but she could walk it.

Hattie once more donned her duster, hat, and riding boots. She stepped outside into the autumn sunlight and welcomed the cool wind that blew the edges of her coat open. She knew John would be checking the herd or riding the property line, and Glen was under strict orders not to do anything more strenuous than sit on his small front porch. He wasn't there when Hattie walked past the cabin, and she hoped he was resting.

Glen had been a godsend after her husband felt it his duty to leave and fight in the war, but he was a man who had said goodbye to youth long before he came to work for the McBrides. It wasn't the first time Hattie had worried about him, and it wouldn't be the last. Hattie walked on familiar paths over the pastures, past the horses, and along the spring-fed creek that assured her animals would always have plenty of water. Hattie closed her eyes. The crisp air caressed her smooth skin and threatened to blow her hat away. She didn't care. Out here on the land, she was free to be herself, and she relished in that freedom.

The ground shook beneath Hattie's feet. The earth moved, an occurrence which Hattie had heard about in stories but never experienced before. It was the echo that reached her ears and the smoke pluming from the base of the mountain that stunned Hattie, but only for a second. She lifted the edges of her skirt, and her strong legs carried her across the fields. The smoke billowed above the pines, and Hattie increased her speed, pain shooting up through her arm with every jarring step.

"Hattie!"

The shout came only seconds before the rumbling. Hattie fell forward, her hands breaking her fall before her head collided with a rock. She grabbed her wounded shoulder and rolled over onto her side to relieve the pressure. Her eyes closed against the searing pain. She heard thundering hooves covering the land at great speed, while her name was shouted over and over again.

"Hattie!"

Warm arms encompassed her body, and Hattie shook her head to clear her vision and thoughts. "Carson."

Carson lifted her until she stood steady on her own feet.

"The mountain. Smoke."

"I know." Carson lifted her chin and made an examination of her face, turning her head to the right then the left. He then carefully patted down her arms. "Are you hurt?"

Hattie's ears started to ring. "What?"

"Are you hurt?" Carson answered his own question a second later. "You're bleeding. The stitches must have pulled." Without preamble, he lifted her onto the back of his horse and swung up behind her.

Hattie watched the landscape bounce and shift until Carson pulled the horse to a stop in front of her house. Glen raced over, his good arm swinging above his head.

"Did you see John?" Glen asked.

The fog over Hattie's mind began to clear. "No. Do you know where he went this morning?"

Glen exhaled in rapid breaths. "Rounding up the last of the strays."

Carson lowered Hattie to the ground and without a word turned his horse. Man and animal raced toward the dwindling smoke.

HATTIE WATCHED THE minutes tick by on the clock. Fifteen minutes. Thirty. Forty-Five. She didn't have to glance out the window to know that the smoke had dissipated or that men from town had joined Carson in the search for John. She passed the window every few minutes in her pacing. Casey stopped by long enough to tell her that the blast had been heard all the way in town and more than a dozen men were now at the mountain. Emma was on her way with the wagon, he'd said, but the seconds continued to tick by until Emma arrived with supplies.

"Do they know how bad it is?" Emma asked.

Hattie shook her head and continued to pace. Emma left her alone and joined Glen in the kitchen. They continued to wait until Hattie decided she'd waited long enough.

Riders. Hattie hurried to the front door and swung it open, bumping her arm in her haste. Carson rode in front, leading John's horse—without John. Hattie rushed down the porch steps and as the men approached and slowed their mounts, she saw that John sat in front of Casey. The young man's head lolled to one side, his eyes closed, his arms limp.

"No, not John!"

Carson dismounted and lifted Hattie out of the way, then took her place beside Casey's horse. With extreme care, and no haste, Casey lowered young John into Carson's strong arms and then dismounted. Together they carried John into the house. Hattie's gaze drifted to the men from town who remained on their horses. Each one's face portrayed the same grimness as the sheriff when he'd arrived at her ranch to tell her that her husband had died.

Hattie covered the distance to the front door in a few long strides, her steps faltered as she approached the kitchen. Voices carried to her before she reached the crowded room. John was laid out on the long wooden table in the center of the kitchen. He didn't move, not so much as a twitch. Hattie knew this because her eyes never left John's face. Emma hovered low over the young man and pressed the end of a stethoscope to his chest.

"Emma?"

Her friend flashed her eyes to Hattie, but then returned her attention to John. Carson was the one to move to Hattie's side and wrap his arm around her waist. She didn't object. She needed the comfort his strength provided. Had Samuel been laid on a table like this, or had he been in a hospital tent? Or did he die immediately and left on the battlefield until the wounded had been carried away? Hattie didn't know the details of her husband's death, and she hadn't wanted to know.

John's chest and arms looked ravaged. Casey pressed cloths down over the worst of the injuries and held them in place. Hattie knew the moment when it was too late to help him. Emma slowly pulled her stethoscope away and brushed the palm of her hand over John's cheek.

HATTIE STEPPED OUTSIDE of the small cabin where Glen and John had made their home.

"You didn't have to be the one to tell him."

Hattie raised her eyes to Carson's. "Emma would have told him, but John was my family. I don't know what Glen will do without him."

"Glen still has you."

Even in gratitude, Hattie couldn't manage a smile. "Until the day I die." When Carson stepped closer and opened his arms to her, Hattie fell against his chest, her head tucked beneath his chin. Several minutes passed before Carson inched away and suggested they walk.

"There isn't going to be a good time to tell you what we found."

Hattie stopped halfway to the corrals. Revenge consumed her, but it was determination for justice that kept her steady. "I want to know."

"The blast caused an avalanche, just enough to loosen some larger rocks. John was half buried when we found him."

Hattie didn't turn away from Carson's gaze. "What purpose was there to set the dynamite off by the mountain? An avalanche wouldn't be guaranteed to harm anyone."

"Could be they kept watch on your place, waited for the right moment."

Carson resumed their walk until they reached the barn. No one else was around. Glen's oldest friend, who worked at the livery in town and rode with the men who found John, sat with him in the cabin. Emma and Casey had returned to town with John's body. The other men who had joined in the search announced that they would take shifts keeping watch at the ranch. However, Carson sent them home to their families. Another time she might have taken issue with his highhandedness, but right now she was grateful for the privacy. If she was going to cry, she'd rather not have an audience.

"What else, Carson? Where did you go when you left here yesterday?"

Carson leaned against the corral fence. "To Buckman's ranch."

Hattie sucked in a sharp breath. "You shouldn't have done that."

"Someone had to." Carson held up a hand before she could retort. "And you couldn't make the ride without further injuring yourself." He nodded to her shoulder. "Emma fixed the stiches."

Hattie nodded. "What happened at Buckman's?"

"He wasn't there. He passed away last week and his son, Hollis, is running the operation."

"We would have heard about a death like that, and I didn't know he had a son."

Carson shrugged. "Not if Buckman Jr. didn't want the word to get out yet, which seemed to be the case. I hadn't heard of a son, either, and I'd guess the old man kept Hollis under close watch. Crazy Eyes is what my mother would have called him. He's weak-minded, but has the men and money to do whatever he wants."

"You think Hollis Buckman did all of this?"

"I don't think he would pull the trigger, but I don't doubt he sent his men to handle things."

Hattie shook her head. "To what end?"

Carson pointed two fingers at his eyes. "Crazy. If you look straight into his eyes, there's more than one man in there and not all of them good."

"You believe in that?"

Carson didn't flinch when he looked straight at her. "Of course. Too many unexplainable events and behaviors in life not to believe in the . . . unusual."

"Well, crazy or not, I need proof that he was behind this or the marshal won't touch him. The Buckman's are too powerful, or at least the elder was."

"You don't need proof to create suspicion."

Hattie narrowed her eyes at Carson. "What exactly do you have planned?"

Carson's gaze followed the lines of her body and then steadied on her face. "How's the shoulder feeling?"

"I'll live."

"You still can't ride."

"So you and Emma continue to tell me."

Carson's lips curved into the barest hint of a smile. "But you could manage in the wagon."

HATTIE STARED AT the expansive valley dotted with cabins, barns, and outbuildings. In the center of what could have been a small village stood a massive house. When Jade Buckman bought this land at the beginning of the war, he didn't waste any time building his empire. Buckman built his wealth in mining, but word was he wanted to become one of the great cattle barons of the new Montana Territory. He'd lived long enough to see the dream begin, but it might be considered lucky that he wouldn't be around to see his empire crumble.

"You sent word to the marshal?"

Carson nodded. "Casey will see it done."

"For a man who rarely leaves his mountain, you make friends quickly."

Carson's shadowed eyes looked her way. "Not as easily as you might think. Some people are just worth the effort." He faced forward again and leaned back into the buckboard chair. "Are you ready for this?"

"I'm ready."

It didn't take them long to descend the hill into the valley where Buckman's land seemed to reach from one end of the earth to the other. Three riders approached from the sides, but Carson didn't slow the wagon nor did he speed the horses' pace.

"Boss told you not to come back, half-breed."

"Best turn back on around before you give us cause to shoot you."

Hattie glanced at Carson to gauge his reaction to the men's words, but he continued to stare straight ahead. He did reach out and squeeze her hand, though the action did little to reassure her.

"You hear me, half-breed?"

One of the men stopped his horse in front of the wagon just as they'd reached the first outbuilding in the cropping of cabins. Carson sensed that Hattie recognized the stranger from outside the clinic, and leaned toward her, "Your stranger in the street."

"Was he here before?"

Carson shook his head. "Likely seeing if you pulled through." He then looked up at the man who spoke with bravado. "You won't want to do that, Murphy."

The man pulled his pistol from its holster and pointed it directly at Carson. "I think I might want to do a bit more than that. The way I figure, I kill you and we get her."

"Remember what happened the last

time you tried to draw on me."

The man's smirk disappeared.

Carson continued. "You want to tell these boys about the card game at Fort Bridger or should I?"

One of the other men called out, "What's he talkin' about, Murph?"

Murphy hesitated and then lowered his weapon. "None of your business." Murphy holstered his pistol. "I reckon the boss'll want to see you after all."

Carson flicked the reins and set the pair of horses back in motion. He seemed to ignore the men riding beside them, but Hattie couldn't. For all her grit, this was not her ranch and these weren't the kind folks of Crooked Creek. She inched closer to Carson and followed his lead by ignoring the men. They pulled to a stop in front of the massive house they'd seen from the hill. Leaning against one of the hitching posts was a small man, no taller than herself. He bore a slight resemblance to the late Jade Buckman, but where Jade stood tall with broad shoulders and possessed an air of authority, this man appeared inconsequential.

Hollis Buckman pointed to the spot on the ground in front of him. Carson simply stared at the man and remained in the wagon.

"You've failed again, Hollis."

"I don't know what you mean, but I sure do appreciate you bringing along fairer company this time."

Carson's lips remained in a straight line and had not Hattie sensed the energy reverberating from his body, she might have thought him bored.

"Which one of your boys set the fuse, Hollis?"

Hollis pushed away from the hitching post and focused on Hattie. "I did hear about your troubles, ma'am, and I swear to you that I will find the man who would dare harm such a beautiful creature."

Crazy Eyes. That's what Carson said his mother would have called Hollis Buckman. Had Hattie not seen it for herself, she might not have believed one man could appear to be so many. His thinning, dull-brown hair and narrow eyes set too close together did little to help his appearance. Hollis shifted flirtatious eyes away from her and focused eyes filled with hatred, as black as the coal buried beneath the earth. His voice changed, and he slapped the side of his leg with one hand. He whooped and hollered and drew his gun. The single shot echoed through the valley before he holstered it again.

"I think we could have a little fun. I insist you and your lovely companion stay as my guests."

Carson leaned forward, almost blocking Hollis's view of Hattie. "Mrs. McBride will have your apology and the name of the men you sent to try and kill her and the men who lit the fuse and killed the boy."

Hollis's demeanor quickly changed, and the man with coal-black and evil eyes returned. "You'll get off that wagon or my men will shoot you off."

Carson looked to each man who either sat a horse or stood nearby. Murphy held onto the handle of his pistol, but no man drew a weapon.

Hollis drew his gun, but not before Carson drew and fired, bringing Hollis to the ground. Crazy Eyes was no more, for Hollis's beady eyes now opened wide, and Hattie would have sworn she saw fear cross the younger Buckman's dirt-covered face.

"You don't want to do that, Murphy." Carson steadied his gun on the only man who appeared to be a threat. "Who lit the fuse?"

One of the younger men who first approached them with Murphy called out, "It was Murph who done it. He's the only been gone from the ranch in a week."

Carson's gaze didn't waver from Murphy. "Any of you boys want a good word in with the marshal, you'll get Murphy's gun and tie him up in the back of the wagon."

Three men were quick to do Carson's bidding, but the others stared beyond them to the hill. Hattie turned in the wagon seat and peered over Carson's shoulder. A dozen men and their horses crested the hill above the valley. Front and center stood Casey Latimer, and beside him, most of the men from Crooked Creek.

Hattie swiveled back to look at Carson. "You knew they were coming?"

Carson shrugged. "There was a chance the marshal wouldn't get here in time."

The men had Murphy bound and hoisted into the back of one of the Buckman's wagons. Casey and the others rode down the hill, and every other man held up their hands and stepped back, indicating they weren't a threat.

Carson holstered his gun, though Hattie didn't recall how it managed to get from his hip to his hand so quickly. Hattie's eyes drifted from Carson to the man on the ground and the dark pool of blood seeping into the hard-packed dirt.

"**Did you take** me out there knowing you'd kill him?"

Carson pulled the wagon and team to a stop halfway between the Buckman's ranch and Crooked Creek.

"I'd hoped it wouldn't come to that, especially with you there, but I wasn't going to give him the chance to put another bullet in you."

"I don't understand. Then why bring me at all?"

Carson draped the reins over his thigh and faced Hattie. "Justice. You deserved to face the man who tried to kill you, who killed John, and tried to take your ranch. Was I wrong?"

"No, you weren't wrong. It's just not what I expected."

Carson's fingers cupped her chin and turned her head back around to face him. "It never is."

"How did they know you were a half-breed?" Hattie almost regretted the question the moment the words escaped her lips.

Carson didn't appear offended, but he did study her in silence for a few moments. "I may not look it, but people talk. Once they know, it's like a brand you can't wash off."

Hattie chose to return to a more comfortable subject. "What will happen to Murphy?"

Carson dropped his hand to his lap. "That'll be up to a judge and jury, but he'll probably hang. Does that bother you?"

"It should." Hattie faced forward and pointed toward home. Carson followed suit and set the team back in motion. "It should bother me, but God help me, it doesn't."

Hattie had cried herself to sleep that

night, and in the morning when she woke, Carson was asleep in a chair by her bed. She hadn't heard him enter her room, nor had she realized he remained in the house after she assured him that all she needed was sleep. Now, Hattie watched him through half-raised eyes and noticed for the first time the stubble on his cheeks and the dark circles under his eyes. A man she didn't know until a few days ago had become a great champion and protector.

When Hattie's gaze returned to Carson's face, she found him looking directly at her. He didn't smile, didn't move, but what looked like pale blue halos circled the black center of his eyes. Hattie blinked a few times before looking again. No halos, just her weary eyes demanding sleep. She gave into the fatigue and closed her eyes once more.

When Hattie awakened again, she was alone in the room. For a moment, she thought Carson's presence had been an apparition, but the chair which he'd occupied was beside her bed where he left it. She roused her body and mind, testing her wounded arm and shoulder. Tender, but some of the stiffness had ebbed. She checked the stitches and made a mental note to ask Emma when they could come out.

Hattie finished her morning ablution, dressed, and made her way down the stairs. Quiet. Too quiet. With each step down, she sensed the absence of life on the ranch. The tears she'd shed the night before threatened to spill over once again. One man she lost to a war, another to a battle that never should have been fought, and now the only family she had left ached from the loss of his only child.

She would ask Glen to move into the main house with her. Perhaps together, they could find a way to heal and move forward.

Light filtered in through the glass windows as Hattie made her way to the kitchen. The fragrant scent of coffee filled the air and she quickened her pace. Carson stood with a mug in hand and his back to her. He looked at the window, but at what, she could only guess.

"You stayed."

Carson turned. "You're feeling better?"

Hattie nodded. "I slept too long. There are chores to be done, and I don't expect or want Glen working again, at least for a while." Hattie filled a tin mug with the freshly brewed coffee and held up the cup. "Thank you for this."

"Glen and I have seen to the morning chores."

Hattie paused, the mug barely touching her lips. "You what?"

"He was already working when I went out at sunup. Nothing he couldn't handle with his injury, but he insisted."

Hattie exhaled and closed her eyes for a moment. "He should be resting, mourning."

Carson lowered his empty mug to the table and moved closer to where she stood beside the stove. "So should you. I know something of loss, and sometimes a man has to keep moving or he'll fall apart."

Hattie knew too well what Carson meant. After she'd learned Samuel was gone forever, her only solace was the ranch. She lost herself in the work, sweat, and finally the tears. Then she picked herself up and got back to work.

"I appreciate you helping out this

morning." Hattie lifted the mug to her lips again, only to set it down. "That sounded callous, as though saying 'thank you' would be enough. Nothing I could do would ever be enough to repay you."

Carson crossed his arms and leaned against the edge of the stove. "You're going to need more help around here."

Hattie walked to the window and looked out over her land. Tears had been shed, and more would fall and sink into the earth with the sweat and blood that came from toiling on the land. But it was time to get back to work. "I'll find someone."

"You already have." Carson had approached from behind, his footsteps silent.

"How do you do that?"

Carson grinned. "It's the Crow in me."

"Who have I found?"

"Me."

Hattie faced Carson completely now. "Repayment means I do something for you, not the other way around. I'm not your responsibility."

Carson's eyes sparkled and managed to fade the dark circles under his eyes. "We'll have to disagree on that."

Hattie crossed her arms. "That bad habit of yours is coming back, Mr. White Eagle."

Carson's grin dissolved, but the sparkle in his eyes remained. "It's a bad habit I'd like to hold onto for a while. That is, if you can live with it."

Hattie studied the man before her— once a stranger and now a man testing her resolve. She planned to remain a widow, work her land, and be buried beneath the soil she and her husband fought to preserve. They had left the East in search of a grand adventure, and Samuel wouldn't have wanted her to give up on their dreams. But now, she had to make them her dreams. "I can live with that, Mr. White Eagle."

THE END

Thank you for reading "Hattie of Crooked Creek"!

Scroll through to enjoy "Briley of Crooked Creek," the next short story in the Crooked Creek series.

BRILEY OF CROOKED CREEK

MK McCLINTOCK

"I'm not afraid of hard work or a challenge. Some of us simply have no other choice. For now, this is home. I hope there is a small amount of admiration for those who don't back down." —BRILEY DONAGHUE

Far from home and with no family left, Briley Donaghue answers an advertisement from a rancher seeking a wife in Montana Territory. She arrives in Crooked Creek to find an empty cabin, a letter from her fiancé, and too many unanswered questions. Alone and uncertain, Briley forges a new life in an unfamiliar land.

BRILEY OF CROOKED CREEK

Crooked Creek, Montana Territory
December 1865

UNTOUCHED SNOW SURROUNDED the small cabin. A narrow stream of smoke did not rise from the chimney. The small barn tucked away behind the cabin stood in silence, as though its occupants had long abandoned the sturdy structure.

"Are you certain you have the right place, ma'am?"

Briley Donaghue sat perched on the seat of the buckboard next to the older man with a friendly smile who answered to Clete. The stage coach driver had greeted Clete with a grand handshake and broad grin, asking after his wife. The driver assured her that no one would look after her better than Clete, and so she hired him. She had expected her future husband to meet the stage and escort her to the home they would share. At least, that had been the fanciful notion Briley's imagination had concocted when she answered the advertisement. His letters hadn't been filled with romantic gestures nor had she really expected such things from a stranger.

Now that she gazed upon her immediate future, Briley thought that if she'd had any sense at all, she would have found a way to return to Ireland rather than venturing to Montana Territory. "It's the right place." Her voice was filled with apprehension.

Clete jumped down from the driver's perch and hurried to her side of the wagon. With greater ease than Briley expected from the older man, Clete lifted her down. Briley's black leather boots were no match for the deep snow, but Clete walked alongside her until she reached the front door. With a discouraging look first at the door and then at her, Clete returned to the wagon to fetch her belongings.

Briley's gloved hand knocked once, then twice. She gripped the metal latch on the primitive door and pushed inward. A burst of cold and musty air from the dark room greeted her. A few minutes later, Clete joined her inside and set the two bags on the board floor.

"Was someone expecting you?"

Briley walked farther into the room and rested her hand on the back of one of two chairs in the room. A large stone fireplace covered a third of one wall and a shelf filled the space of another. Dust filtered through the air, landing on everything already covered in a thin layer.

"It would seem they weren't." Briley reached for an envelope on the table—it, too, was covered in dust. Her name was scrawled across the front of the faded paper.

"Ma'am?"

Briley turned to Clete. "I'll manage quite well here." She didn't mistake both the concern and hesitation in Clete's eyes and was quick to reassure him. "Not to worry. I'm quite used to country living. Might I call upon you again should I need assistance?"

"Yes, ma'am. I looked around some outside. The wood shed is good and stocked for a few weeks. There ain't no horse in the stable, but there's an old wagon."

Briley didn't know how to ride a horse. However, she would need a horse to pull that wagon. She thought of the limited funds she had brought with her—some her own and some from her husband-to-be. "Is there a place in town where I might purchase a horse?"

"Blacksmith don't have any right now, leastwise that I know, but Miss Hattie sells horses. She lives by the mountain on the other side of town. I'll tell Peyton, uh, Sheriff Sawyer, that you're looking since he goes out that way once a week."

Briley managed a smile for the man. "Thank you, Clete, I'd appreciate that. Would you care for some tea? I brought a tin with me, though it may take a few minutes to boil the water."

"Don't mind if I do, Miss Donaghue." Clete smashed his worn hat atop his head and started for the door. "I got to see to a few things first." Without encouragement or instruction, Clete started a fire in the hearth to take the chill off the room. He then carried in enough wood for at least three days' worth of fires. When Briley thought he was done, Clete stepped back outside and returned ten minutes later with two buckets of water. She had the tea brewed and offered her guest a place at the table. Clete wrapped his hands around the warm tin cup and drank deeply.

"This is mighty good. I thank you."

"It's I who am grateful." Briley sipped her own tea and enjoyed the warm emanating from the hearth. It had been far too long since she'd taken pleasure in simple comforts. "You better get home to your family before dark settles in."

"I reckon so." Clete finished his tea and placed his hat back on his head. "There's a spring down yonder behind the cabin that runs all year. I reckon there's a pump around here, but I can't see one." He stepped outside and returned immediately with a sack tied off at the top. "There's a springhouse, mostly covered in snow, but I smelled the meat and it's good. The place was left good and stocked."

Briley hadn't considered even the smallest of necessities when she assured Clete that she'd be all right alone. "Thank you. You've done more than I could have asked or expected, and I'm grateful. Now, I promise that all is well here." Briley pulled out her money purse, but Clete shook his head and backed away."

"No, Miss Donaghue. You done already paid me for the ride."

"Yes, but this is for—"

"My place is a few miles east. I'll be

looking in on you again." Clete tipped his hat and sauntered from the cabin.

Briley stood in the silence, the occasional crackle from the fire filling the void.

PEYTON SAWYER CONSIDERED himself a patient and understanding man most of the time. This was not one of those times. "You'll stay in there until I see fit, and if you ask again, I'll guarantee you don't get out of there until spring." Peyton swung the door closed and stepped into his office. The door to the office opened from the outside and in swept Clete Foster and a gust of frigid air.

Clete brushed the snow off his coat. "Beggin' pardon, Sheriff."

"Don't beg for anything, Clete." Peyton rubbed a hand over his dark beard. "Coffee?"

Clete nodded. "Don't mind if I do, thank you."

Peyton poured a stream of steaming dark liquid into a clean mug and handed it to his visitor. He forced himself not to return to the back cell when the yelling began. Instead, he ignored the shouts and focused on Clete. "Weren't you just in town yesterday?"

"I was at that. You see, Sheriff, I came to tell you—"

The racket became a chorus of screams and rattling of the bars. "Ignore it," Peyton said. "What did you want to tell me?"

Clete grinned. "You got them Teeter brothers in there again?"

"The bane of my existence." Peyton excused himself for a minute and when he returned, silence followed with him. "They care more about their supper than their indignation."

"I reckon they would, seeing as how ain't no two bigger men in these parts. Exceptin' you, of course, and I reckon Mr. Latimer."

Peyton raised a brow and settled himself in the chair behind his desk, his long legs crossed beneath the desk. "Now, what's on your mind, Clete?"

"You see, a lady hired me at the stage stop yesterday to drive her home."

Peyton waited for whatever Clete had felt necessary to rush over in a storm and tell him. "You hire out all of the time."

"I do, Sheriff, that I do, but you see this lady was alone. We got to the cabin, and I reckon she was expectin' someone to be there."

Peyton rose, catching on to Clete's concern. "No one was there."

"Not a soul. She had it all written out on

a paper where she was supposed to go. I didn't feel right leaving her there, but she said she was staying. She has a nice way about speaking like old Mr. Sweeney did, but she's real music-like. I done what I could, but it ain't proper or right for a nice lady like her to be alone. I promised I'd check up on her again, but I figure you ought to know. And, she needs a horse, Sheriff. If I was a speculating man, I'd say she didn't—"

Peyton's hand rose, effectively cutting off Clete's rambling. "Where did you drive her?"

"That old cabin west of town before you get to the big meadow. It's right there on Crooked Creek. Her name is Miss Donaghue. .. how about that, I didn't get her Christian name."

Peyton glanced at the clock. It was late enough in the morning to make an unexpected visit. "I appreciate you bringing me this information. You did right by Miss Donaghue. Would you do something else for me?"

"I sure will."

"Find Casey Latimer—you might look first at Doc Hawkins's clinic—and ask him to check in on the brothers while I ride out."

"Right away, Sheriff." Clete smashed his hat back on his head of thin brown hair, pulled the collar up on his thick coat, and stepped back into the cold.

OWING HER THANKS to Clete, Briley had survived her first night at the cabin. Her father would have called her impulsive decision a foolish one. What had compelled her to exhibit such rash behavior? What had her husband-to-be thought when he left her behind without a proper explanation? She read the letter again and brushed it aside, anger and disappointment not allowing her to fully understand what her intended had meant.

"Well, I'm here for now." She placed her fisted hands on her hips and looked around. There wasn't much to examine, but she found a fairly clean bucket that she designated for household chores, not wishing to use the water pails. She managed to unearth a few rags from a trunk and began to remove what dust she could from the cabin.

Briley made quick work of the dusting, and despite the cold, hanged the linens from the bed on a line outside that had been strung from a corner of the cabin to a nearby tree. If nothing else, they'd at least be aired out until she could procure more water from the creek to wash them with the cake of soap she'd brought with her. With water buckets in hand, Briley reached for the door handle.

The knock at the front door startled her enough to drop the buckets, but caution took over. She waited for whoever was on the other side to leave.

"Miss Donaghue? It's Sheriff Sawyer."

Briley expelled the breath she'd been holding and inched open the door. She stared into the shearling-covered chest of a man who stood just beyond the threshold. She stepped back and tilted her head so she could look up at him.

"Miss Donaghue?"

Briley nodded. "Is something wrong, Sheriff?"

He looked over her shoulder—an easy feat—and into the cabin. "Clete mentioned that he drove you out here yesterday and thought you might be expecting someone to meet you here."

Briley gripped the handle on the door if for no other reason than something to occupy her nervous hand. "I was expecting someone, though I've since learned he won't be arriving."

"This is Christopher Smith's cabin, Miss Donaghue. Is that who you planned to meet?"

Briley nodded and took a step back, curious eyes on the sheriff.

"I'm sorry to say that Christopher passed away. We received word little more than a month back. I have to ask what you're doing in here."

Briley closed her eyes and then retrieved the letter from the mantel. "Christopher left this for me. I had anticipated arriving weeks ago, but I was held up in New York. I wrote to him of my delay, to which he replied I was still to come."

Peyton steadied his eyes on her for a moment and then accepted the folded letter. He read the few lines quickly and swore under his breath.

"We began corresponding a month before the war ended. I'm sorry to hear of his death. How did it happen?"

Peyton handed the letter back to Briley. "Hold onto that. It will serve as Christopher's last will. He was thrown from his horse and broke his neck, I'm afraid. Christopher got it in his mind to join one of the campaigns out west and fight with them."

"There was no one left to fight."

Peyton's eyes narrowed slightly, and Briley wondered how much he could learn about her from only one glance. "There's always a fight brewing somewhere when people are too greedy to leave well enough alone. In this case, he was joining the army to—" Peyton ground out the next words, "—tame the Indians."

Briley knew the extent to which people would go to do away with those who were different. Had she and her family not left those struggles—the hatred—behind in Ireland? America was supposed to be different, except the war between the North and South had shown her that no country, no matter how free, is immune from conflict. She had hoped the great frontier she'd heard stories about would be different.

When she continued to remain silent, Peyton asked, "How well did you know Christopher?"

Briley had the decency to blush. "Only what he told me in his letters. We corresponded for almost six months, but

I was to meet him here for the first time."

Understanding filled Peyton's deep brown eyes and his features softened.

Briley pressed on before he could comment. "I know he cared for an ill father which is why he didn't join the army during wartime. Instead, he operated a small farm." She looked around the cabin. "At least that's what he said."

"His father passed almost six months back, and there are some crops underneath the snow somewhere, but he wasn't much of a farmer or rancher. If I may be so bold as to remark, I'm not sure Christopher could have supported a wife, though he probably would have tried."

"We hadn't married yet."

"I figured." Peyton stepped back and studied the cabin. "According to the letter, this homestead is yours, so that's something. Although, I don't suppose I can convince you to move into town for the winter."

Briley considered her meager funds. She barely had enough for the supplies she'd need through the winter. She then had to decide if she was going to stay put or find a way back to Ireland. It wouldn't be her first lean winter, and her father had raised a resilient daughter. "I appreciate your concern, but I'll make do here."

Peyton studied her again with his inscrutable gaze. "Christopher had a wagon, and we can get you a horse. Do you know how to drive?"

"I'll learn." Briley watched Peyton watch her, his eyes skimming the length of her gray, wool dress and her worn, black boots. She saw nothing in his eyes that conveyed pity, and yet, she experienced the sudden urge to squirm beneath his gaze.

"Clete said he'd be stopping by again when he returns home from town."

"I'm grateful, but it's not necessary. You've already saved him the bother."

Peyton's lips quirked and he leveled his eyes to hers. "It is, Miss Donaghue, and once Clete fixes an idea in his mind, it doesn't shake loose.

Briley considered every possible reply; they all sounded ungrateful. "Then I shall see Clete later today."

AS PROMISED, CLETE stopped at the cabin on his way home, this time bearing gifts. "It was figured you'd be needing some supplies until you get that horse for your wagon." Clete hefted a wooden crate inside and returned to the wagon for a second box. "These should do for a spell."

More than a spell, Briley thought. "Who figured I would need these supplies."

"Well, don't you?" Clete tugged his wool cap off his head.

Flour, sugar, a few spices, soda, some canned goods, and that was just in the first crate. "I can't accept these."

Clete scratched his scruffy chin. "That's a bit perplexing." He looked around her small, bare kitchen. "How 'bout some of that tea? I think I'm taking a shine to it. Ought to tell the missus."

So, they sat and enjoyed a cup of tea as Clete talked about going home to what he described as a small farm and a saint of a wife who continued to love him after twenty-three years. Briley listened to his stories about his own arrival in Crooked Creek more than twenty years ago.

"I had no idea the town would be so

young. The villages in my own country are centuries old."

"Ain't that something." Clete finished the tea and Briley regretted not something more substantial to offer her new friend. "Lots of towns out this way are younger than what I reckon you're used to." He scratched his chin through the dark beard laced with strands of gray. "You ain't the first Irish that's been through these parts, but I reckon you're the only one here now. Hattie McBride— I reckon it's Hattie White Eagle now—her people are from over that way, but she ain't got that sweet accent like you."

Briley looked into the flames burning low in the hearth, while memories clamored through her thoughts. "I traveled with my family from Ireland before your civil war began."

"It ain't what you expected when you

arrived?" Clete asked.

Briley shook her head. "Unfortunately, no, but we made it work." She rose and offered him another cup of tea.

Clete also rose and stuffed his hat on his head. "I thank you, but I best be getting home. I sure do appreciate the refreshment."

She walked him to the door, silently grateful that he wouldn't linger. She needed time and quiet to process the barrage of memories she had fought so hard to leave buried back in New York.

Clete settled on the seat of the wagon and looked at her. "I'll be seeing you again real soon."

"Please, that won't be. . ." Briley smiled at Clete's lopsided grin. "I look forward to your visit, and I hope I'll have the pleasure of meeting your wife soon."

"She'd like that. She surely would."

Clete's grin broadened. "You have a good night, now."

Briley sighed and watched Clete and his wagon disappear into the fading light.

THE FIRST CRACK followed by a soft pounding roused Briley from a perfectly good slumber—the first she'd had since leaving New York. The second crack and more pounding brought her fully awake. She pushed aside the bed coverings she'd managed to clean in a bucket and dry from a rope in front of the fire. Though frayed in some places, the quilts had offered her warmth and comfort during the cold night.

Her bare feet hit the wood floor, and she immediately pulled them back beneath the covers. She took a moment to focus her eyes in the dimly room and reached for the thick stockings she had set aside the evening before. The heavy wool shawl that she had made back in Ireland enveloped her fully, and when sufficiently covered, she padded across the floor to glance out the window.

The sun had peeked over the mountains, casting vibrant hues of yellow and orange through the sky. Dark clouds now threatened to overtake them, and Briley suspected snow would soon follow. She moved to another window and scanned the area by the small barn behind the cabin. There in the morning light, a man raised his arms above his head and swung down, splitting the log with apparent ease.

Briley watched as he sliced through log after log, adding to the small pile quickly growing. Her guest must have sensed he was being watched because he lowered the ax and stared directly at her. Briley's first instinct was to step away from the window, but she held her ground and waved. He waved back.

Briley stepped away from the window. She dropped the shawl and splashed water on her face, and then busied herself getting dressed. Her new food stores allowed her to mix together fresh scones—a staple in her home back in Ireland—and a fresh loaf of bread. She made a mental note to do a complete inventory today of the springhouse Clete had mentioned.

The chopping ceased and a short time later, when the sheriff didn't knock on the front door, Briley stepped outside. He was feeding his horse a handful of oats from his saddlebag. Without turning away from his horse, he said, "I should apologize for the early hour, Miss Donaghue."

"No apology needed. It wasn't—"

"If you're going to say it wasn't necessary to chop the wood, please don't." He turned to face her then. "It's what's done here."

Images of the quaint village where she'd grown up flashed through her mind. Neighbors helping neighbors was a concept she'd almost forgotten since arriving in this country. "Then let me thank you with some breakfast. It's a light repast but should see you back to town." Briley waited and almost wondered if he would graciously refuse her offer. Instead, he nodded.

"I'd like that, thank you." Peyton smoothed his hand over the neck of his dark bay gelding. He stomped the snow from his boots before entering her now tidy cabin. She smiled and pointed to a washbasin on the counter when he held up his hands.

After he was seated, she placed the plate of fresh-from-the-oven scones on the scarred surface of the table. Briley had unearthed a trunk of linens and decided her task for that day would be to launder them and see what she could use for a table covering. "I'm afraid I have only tea prepared, but I could brew some coffee."

"Tea is just fine, thank you."

She felt his gaze on her as she moved about the cooking area. He didn't reach for the food until she sat down and offered it to him.

"These smell heavenly." Peyton spread some of the preserves over the scone. His eyes closed briefly. "And taste even better."

Briley enjoyed watching him savor the first scone and then the second. When the last crumb was off his plate, she said, "Clete came by again yesterday, just as you said he would. The supplies were unexpected, though I suspect that wasn't Clete's doing."

Peyton grinned and sampled his tea. "He'll stop by regular now. Were the supplies not what you needed?"

"Yes, they were, and I'm truly grateful, but I hope you can understand that I need to pay you back."

Peyton smiled and leaned back slightly. "I can understand that." Peyton remembered what it was like to make his own way, and though he had his theories about stubborn women, he respected her more for it. He drank deeply of the tea and said, "I'll admit that I'm partial to a strong cup of coffee, but this tea is wonderful and nothing like what I've had around here before."

Briley lowered her own teacup. "I brought it from New York. It's a blend my parents favored when I was young, and I can't seem to go a day without it."

Peyton leaned forward on his arm and gazed at her across the table. "I have to confess that chopping wood wasn't the reason I came out this morning."

Briley leaned back and pulled the edges of her shawl closer together. "I see."

"No, you don't. Christopher Smith—your intended—kept to himself out here. I didn't know much about him except that he was married once and lost his wife and a baby boy during childbirth. Did he tell you any of this in his letters?"

Briley nodded, uncertain why the sheriff would bring this up. "He did."

"You see, Christopher gave up after that and just about lost this place. I wired the bank in Denver that dealt with

Christopher, and they said it was cleared up. He even sent them a letter putting your name on the deed."

Briley exhaled slowly and relaxed her shoulders. "He must have known he was leaving before I even departed New York. He never told anyone else, did he?"

"Not that I've found. Christopher kept to himself. I can't agree with the way he left you alone here, but he did right by you in leaving you this place." Peyton finished his tea, eyeing her every so often during the silence. "How did you come to leave New York? If you don't mind me saying, you don't look the type to answer an advertisement for a mail-order bride."

Briley moved to rise and gathered the dishes from the table.

"I didn't mean to offend you, Miss Donaghue."

She put the dishes in the washbasin and

turned around. "You didn't offend me. I'm embarrassed to say that I answered out of desperation."

Peyton rose but remained on his side of the table. "You have no family left?"

"A few cousins in Ireland. Not long after we came to America, war broke out and most of the young men—including my father and brother—joined the Northern Cause."

"Your mother?"

Briley fought back tears. "Losing them cost my mother her hope. She became ill, defeated, and . . . gave up." She brushed back the few tears that managed to escape. "I shouldn't be telling you this, and I don't want pity. Many families lost far more than I did."

"I won't give you pity, though I am sorry for your losses. My cousin, David, died in the war. I was too busy mining in

Colorado to give much thought to it. David and his wife, Emma, lived here in Crooked Creek."

"Is that why you're here, because of your cousin's wife?"

Peyton nodded. "In part. I came up here a few years ago, but I returned to Colorado to finish up some mining business. Sheriff Epps retired this last spring. When I returned to Crooked Creek, I took the job."

"How did you know Christopher?"

"First time I was up here, there was a cave-in. He'd been hunting in the mountains."

"You pulled him out?"

Peyton nodded and then made his way to the front door. "I don't make a habit of talking this much." He lifted his hat and coat from a peg by the door. "I didn't agree with Emma when she decided to stay in their cabin alone. I wanted her to move to town, but I've learned that when a stubborn woman gets an idea in her head, she doesn't back away." He slipped into his coat. "I would still like to convince you to move into town."

Briley's answer was a few seconds in coming. Without a husband and few funds left, she didn't have the luxury of options. "Emma, she made it on her own?"

Peyton sighed and nodded. "She did, though not without some struggles. She's a brave woman."

When he was out the door and his horse's reins were in his hands, Briley asked, "Sheriff Sawyer?"

He turned and waited, his blue eyes seeming to stare right through her. "I'm not afraid of hard work or a challenge. Some of us simply have no other choice.

For now, this is home. I hope there is a small amount of admiration for those who don't back down."

PEYTON WALKED INTO the quiet jailhouse and raised a brow at the man behind the desk. "Are they still alive?"

Casey Latimer stretched his long legs and rose from the chair. "Last I checked. I threatened to starve them if they didn't shut up."

Peyton grinned and hung his hat next to his coat. "That'll do it. I'll give them one more night to think about the errors of their ways. Thanks for watching them again this morning."

Casey shrugged. "Not a problem. Emma has been up with a patient all night anyway. Are you going to tell me about her now?"

Peyton's hand paused halfway to his mouth. He drank deeply and then set the coffee aside. "Briley Donaghue. Heaven save me from stubborn women."

"I rather like mine."

Peyton glanced at Casey with a wry grin. "Emma's tamed some. I haven't told you this before, but I'm glad you found each other. She wouldn't listen to me, and the thought of her out there alone all the time—"

"She had this town." Casey leaned a hip against the wall next to the woodstove. "Emma's stronger than you give her credit for."

"No," Peyton laughed. "I've always known how capable and determined she is, I just might have wished it otherwise."

"Why's that?"

Peyton considered his answer carefully. "My mother was a strong woman, didn't think there was anything she couldn't accomplish. It served her well for a lot of years, especially when she had three children to raise on her own. No matter how many times I'd tell her that I'd take care of the hunting and outside chores after school, she kept trying to do it all on her own. She thought schooling was more important for a boy."

"Your mother cared about you. There's nothing wrong with that."

Peyton continued. "One day while I was at school with my sisters, she went hunting on her own and got caught up in the middle of two hunting parties from different tribes. It wasn't until I was old enough to understand that she was lucky to have caught a stray arrow. Living would have been far worse had either hunting party taken her alive." Peyton shook the memory away.

"Emma isn't your mother. Hell, women like her have helped settle west, and most of them didn't have a choice. Take Hattie. When her husband died, was she supposed to give up and sell her ranch? I'd call that a brave decision."

I don't mind a challenge, Briley had said. "So would I," Peyton said. "I may be overprotective, but that doesn't mean I don't believe these women have what it takes to make it out there. Briley Donaghue came west to marry a stranger, and she's too stubborn, but it's admirable to not give up."

Casey chuckled and pushed away from the wall. "We're all too stubborn, which is probably why we survive out here. Is this about what happened to your mother?"

One shout followed another and soon the Teeter brothers were yelling at each other from their respective cells . . . again.

Peyton grabbed the keys from the desk and slammed into the back room. He unlocked the first cell. "Get out of here, Jeb."

Jeb Teeter stared at him. "What about Pete?"

"Pete's staying here. If you two can't be civil to one another in here, then I can't trust you to be civil out there, now can I?"

"Ah, sheriff, we didn't mean no harm," Pete said. "Me and Jeb is just . . . ah, spirited."

"You're a nuisance. Go on now, Jeb, get out of here."

Jeb looked between Peyton and his brother a few times. "I ought to stay put until you spring Pete."

Peyton unlocked Pete's cell and waited for both brothers to follow him into the front office. "If I have to lock you two up again for fighting in the saloon, I'll wire a judge and let him deal with you. Understand?"

Jeb and Pete hung their heads and nodded. Casey laughed as the brothers left the jail and watched as one pushed the other off the boardwalk. "How long do you expect that to last?"

Peyton tossed the keys on the desk, letting them fall with a loud clatter. "A few hours at least. So long as they take their fight home, I don't care." He settled in the chair behind the desk. "When I came back after David died, and Emma refused to leave their cabin, all I could think about was how she'd end up like my mother."

"She spends every day in town now, just like she did back then, Peyton. Emma told me a week didn't go by when someone wasn't dropping off meat and checking in on her, just as you did for more than two years."

Frustrated, Peyton rose. "I have something to do."

Casey reached out and grabbed Peyton's arm. "Does Miss Donaghue remind you of your mother, too? Is that what this about?"

Peyton pulled away. He couldn't answer the question because he didn't know. His sisters had said he smothered them until they both married, and then he became the brother they remembered from their youth. He had dismissed their words as those from young women who wanted too much freedom, but had they been right? He did know the scars from his childhood, from losing their mother, had remained with him all of these years.

"How's Emma patient?"

Casey sighed heavily. "Fever broke this morning. I'll head over there now."

"Give her my love. I'll be back in later."

"Emma wanted me to invite you to supper on Sunday."

Peyton looked back at Casey, a friend and the man who had won Emma's heart. At the time, he believed Casey had saved Emma from the dangers befallen a woman alone in the wilderness. Except now, he understood that Emma didn't need saving.

"I'd like that," Peyton said and left the jail.

BRILEY STUDIED THE two empty stalls in the barn and decided she needed that horse and cursed herself for once again forgetting to ask the sheriff about Hattie's ranch. Such a purchase would consume a good portion of her funds, but not having a means to travel to and from town would be far more detrimental. Her weaving loom and supplies had been left with a family in New York who promised to keep them until she could send funds to ship the loom west. Until that could happen, she would need a job. It would be months before she could start a garden, grow her own food, and begin replenishing her food stores.

"Briley."

She spun around at the soft sound of her name on Peyton's lips. It had been only a few hours since he had left, and strangely, she had felt a keen sense of loss when he rode away. Briley was used to family, laughter, and music filling the air. No matter how lean the years or difficult the harvest, her family and the village always came together to celebrate life. Even when the famine drove so many others away, her family had persevered a decade longer before her parents decided to follow so many others to America. The silence now was overwhelming, and a friendly face had never been as welcome.

"You startled me, is all. It's quiet here, which is why I'm pleased for another visit so soon."

Peyton nodded and walked toward her, his horse trailing behind him. "I wanted to apologize for my words this morning."

Briley's deep brown eyes held his. "I don't recall you saying anything untoward, Sheriff."

"It's Peyton, and it's not my place to tell you how to live."

"Very well, Peyton. I wasn't upset with you, and I do appreciate your concern." Briley walked past him. "Would you like a cup of tea?"

Peyton secured his horse and followed her back to the house. A fire burned strong in the hearth. A heavy cast iron pot over the fire released steam from beneath the lid. A loaf of bread sat on the table, and the contents from a trunk were laid out on the bed. The whole room appeared free of dust and smelled of the fresh pine-scented, winter air that could only be captured by opening windows. "You're settling in."

"Yes, I am." She smiled, looking around at her accomplishments. "There's still much to do, but I enjoy the work." She motioned him to one of the chairs at the table. "Is the town of Crooked Creek in safe hands when you're not there?"

Peyton raised a brow and smiled. "Is my company that awful?"

Briley took his words as he meant them; a playful way to ease the tension left over from that morning. "You're a pleasant diversion." She returned the pot to the cookstove and sat down with her own cup of tea. "Clete had mentioned someone named Hattie who could sell me a horse. Might you tell me where she lives?"

"Too far on foot. I can drive you out there."

Briley couldn't continue to be dependent upon others, and at this rate Peyton and Clete were going to spend more time with her than at their own homes. A horse was her first step to severing the burden they'd hoisted upon themselves. "I would be grateful, thank you."

THE DRIVE TO Hattie's place the following morning was cold but not unpleasant from the seat of Peyton's wagon. It offered Briley an opportunity to see more of the countryside. Despite the thick carpet of snow covering most of the land, the raw beauty shined through. Mountain peaks rolled into one another as they climbed higher and jutted into the sky. Heavy forests of pine and trees she didn't recognize spanned as far as she could see. On the other side of the trees, and too far in the distance to hear the water, she could see a great river weaved a path through the frosty earth.

"What is that river called?"

"The Yellowstone. Hattie's land stretches almost to the banks of that river."

"Is that how the water comes in to Crooked Creek?"

Peyton shook his head and pulled the team to a stop. He jumped down and removed a fallen tree limb off the road, and then returned to the wagon. "Crooked Creek comes down from the mountains and runs alongside the town and through some of the small farms and ranches."

They drove another mile before the ranch came into view. The cabin was almost double in size of Briley's, and not much farther away stood a barn nearly three times the size of the cabin.

"Hattie and her husband raised cattle, but her love has always been horses. Her first husband died in the war. She and Carson White Eagle—her new husband— plan to expand the horse operation."

"White Eagle?"

Peyton nodded. "Carson is half Mountain Crow and half Irish."

"I heard the term half-breed before, but it had been used with such derision." When she sensed Peyton stiffen, she placed a hand on his arm. "I mean no disrespect. The Irish are quite familiar with condemnation, and I harbor no such feelings toward anyone."

"I apologize. Carson is a friend. He doesn't look any different than you or me, but not everyone who passes through are understanding." Peyton pulled the team to a stop in front of the cabin and helped Briley down. A woman with light hair and brilliant green eyes stepped outside. The faint scent of meal over a fire wafted from inside.

"Sheriff." The woman stepped down from the covered porch.

"Afternoon Hattie, this is Miss Briley Donaghue, the new owner of Christopher Smith's homestead, and she's in need of a horse."

Hattie's wide smile brightened her eyes. Briley couldn't help but return the smile.

"You've come to the right place. Carson is out with the mustang herd right now, but you'll meet him soon, I'm sure." Hattie held out her hand when Briley was close enough. "It's nice to meet you."

"The pleasure is mine, and please call me Briley."

Hattie's flaxen curls fell to one side as she studied Briley. "You still have the sound of the old country in you."

Briley nodded. "I've been here five years now."

"I've been here since I was a girl. I'm afraid I lost the Irish in my voice a long time ago. Why don't we take a look at the horses, and then we'll enjoy a bit of refreshment."

It had been ages since Briley sat down with a woman of her age who wasn't as broken as she. "That sounds lovely, thank you."

Hattie gathered her coat and hat from inside. As they fell into step beside

Hattie, Briley noticed that Peyton slowed his stride to match hers, and Hattie followed suit. They stepped up to a corral attached to the barn where half a dozen beautiful horses waited.

"What are you looking for in a horse?"

Briley glanced at Hattie. Her family had a plow horse back home and another they used for the wagon to go back and forth to town, but she'd only ridden a few times. "Gentle. I'm afraid I'm not a good rider. I do have a wagon and need to be able to travel to and from town."

"I have a strong mare who would do well for you, and she's gentle enough if you decide to ride."

Briley stood beside Peyton and watched Hattie expertly cut a horse from the group, though she didn't have to do much. The animals remained still as Hattie walked among them. She placed a halter and lead rope on one and guided the animal outside of the corral. Peyton secured the fence while Hattie tied the black-and-white spotted horse to the rail.

"She's beautiful." And, Briley thought, too expensive.

Hattie ran her hand along the mare's back. "She has a good constitution and a gentle spirit. She'll do well for you."

Briley reached a tentative hand out and held it just below the mare's nose. After a few heavy breaths, the mare nickered and nudged Briley's hand.

"She likes you." Hattie exchanged a grin with Peyton.

Peyton said, "Would you mind adding a little feed to the purchase, Hattie? Just enough to get her through today and tomorrow?"

"Not a problem."

Briley missed the exchange between

Hattie and Peyton, but when Hattie walked into the barn, Briley faced Peyton. "This is a fine horse, but I'm afraid she'll be more than I can afford right now."

"Hattie's prices are fair, don't worry." Peyton untied the mare and led her to his wagon. He returned in time to heft the small sack of feed from Hattie's arms and carried that to the wagon as well.

Briley watched the mare bob her head in anticipation for the ride, and despite the practical voice in her mind telling her to walk away, she turned to Hattie. "She's a magnificent horse, Hattie, thank you. What do I owe you?"

Hattie's green eyes narrowed for a second and then she smiled. "Let's have that cup of tea first."

An hour later, Peyton drove the wagon away from Hattie's ranch with Briley's new mare tied the back. A price had been given—a far too reasonable price—and the transaction completed. Once they returned to Briley's cabin, Peyton gave her a quick lesson on how to hitch the horse to the wagon. The small wagon cart her family had owned did not weigh nearly as much or have quite as many pieces as the larger wagon. They practiced three times before Peyton was confident Briley could manage on her own.

Peyton rummaged through a closed off-area Briley hadn't noticed before and emerged empty handed. "It seems Christopher had only the one saddle he would have taken. I have an extra one that should work."

"I can't possibly accept anything else."

Peyton didn't push the issue, for which Briley was grateful. "Do you know if there is a dressmaker or seamstress in town?"

Peyton guided the mare to one of the two stalls and fed her from the sack of grain Hattie had provided. "You're looking for work?"

Briley nodded. "I'm a fair hand with needle work."

"There's no dressmaker that I know of. I told you about Emma—and her husband, Casey. I'm dining with them on Sunday. Why don't you join us? Emma will be able to steer you to the right people."

PEYTON RODE BACK before the sun began to set. He knew he couldn't spend all of his time out at Briley's cabin and still take care of the town, and yet he spent the ride back figuring out how to do just that. He saw Emma's wagon in front of the clinic but not Casey's horse. He dismounted and secured his horse before stepping inside. Emma always kept the clinic warm and comfortable. The faint scent of lye and beeswax filled the air.

She came down the staircase and paused a few steps from the bottom. "Aren't you a sight."

Peyton leaned in and kissed her cheek. "All I ever need is your smile to brighten my day."

Emma swatted his arm and moved past him into her surgery. "I haven't seen you around today. Casey tells me we have a new resident."

Peyton nodded and made himself comfortable in Emma's desk chair. "Briley Donaghue. She's living in the cabin out at the edge of Crooked Creek."

Emma stopped folding bandages. "Christopher Smith's old cabin?"

"That's the one." Peyton waved away any other potential questions. "I don't know how much she wants folks to know about how she came to be here, so you'll have to put your questions directly to her."

"I'd like to meet her. Would you invite her to supper on Sunday?"

"I'm glad you've asked."

Emma grinned at him. "Because you already invited her."

Peyton's sheepish smile was fleeting. "Emma, did you ever feel as though I pressured you too much after David died?"

Emma had moved onto cleaning her surgical instruments. She laid down narrow clamps he'd seen her use a few times to remove bullets and faced him. "I won't pretend I don't know what you mean. I suppose back then I might have felt that way."

Peyton rose from her chair and sat on the edge of her desk, his arms crossed. "You never said anything."

"David told me once about his cousin who grew up in Colorado and what happened to your mother. When you got word of his death and came north, I was thrilled to have family close by."

Peyton scrubbed a hand over his face. "I didn't realize you knew back then."

"I had enough people against me, including my own family. A woman like me out here alone wasn't entirely unheard of, but I drew plenty of censure in the beginning. At least I understood your reasons."

Peyton took Emma's hands in his own. "I'm sorry for anything I might have said back then, and even more so that I left in anger."

Understanding, and then sympathy, flashed in her eyes. "You left because you couldn't convince me to not live out there alone."

Peyton nodded and released her hands. "Had I known what a cuss I was back then, or if I remembered everything I said to you, I'd have too many apologies to give."

Emma cupped the side of Peyton's face. "No you wouldn't. I love that you cared enough to say and do what you did. Perhaps I needed that in order to strengthen my own resolve. I almost returned home, but the more you pushed, the more I was determined to stand my ground."

Peyton shared a laugh with her over the irony and pulled her into his arms. "Thank you, Emma."

Someone filled the doorway and

cleared their throat. "Surprised you didn't hear me, Sheriff."

Peyton smiled at his friend over Emma's head. "I heard you, Casey." He stepped back and kissed her cheek. "You have a hell of a woman here."

Casey stepped forward and slipped an arm around his wife. "No arguments here."

Emma smiled and said to Peyton, "Please tell Briley supper will be at half past five. I expect you'll be driving her." Her eyes sparkled with a little mischief and a lot of love.

BRILEY HARNESSED THE mare to the wagon as Peyton had shown her. She awakened before the sun, eager for her first drive into the small town of Crooked Creek. Her glimpse of the town when she first arrived had been brief, eager as she was to meet her fiancé. She harbored no guilt for not missing a man she'd never met. Instead, she woke these past few mornings with a deep sense of gratitude for his generosity. He might not have chosen her in the end once they met face-to-face, but he had otherwise done everything a husband-to-be would do for his intended, and then some.

Briley wasn't unused to hard work and unexpected challenges. Life on the modest Irish farm had taught her time offered no guarantees except change and unpredictability. She considered her new life in Crooked Creek as a simple alteration in her plans. She brought with her one wool coat, but the biting cold of the early morning forced her to acknowledge that neither her coat nor her leather boots would suffice for life in Montana.

Beneath her coat she wore two layers of her warmest clothing. One of her wool scarves was wrapped tightly around her neck and tucked into her coat. By the time she finished hitching the wagon, a thin layer of sweat beaded across her brow. She quickly wiped it away and walked the mare outside. Briley brushed her gloved hand over the mare's neck. "You deserve a fine name, that you do. Nessa is what I'll call you. She was a strong and brave female warrior who lived long ago in Ireland. You'll be strong and brave for me, won't you, girl?"

Nessa nickered as though she agreed. Briley loaded her basket into the back of the wagon, climbed up on the seat, and with a deep breath, lightly flicked the reins.

She followed the same road on which Clete had driven her a week before. Briley enjoyed the light fall of snow as she and the mare made their way along the road to town. The thick, white flakes settled on the earth and covered her path as the wheels rolled over and over. A gentle breeze sent some of the snowflakes into a swirl. "A lovely sight to be sure, Nessa." The mare ambled along while Briley enjoyed the peace of her surroundings. A heavy curtain of snow began to form all around them, and the forested quieted until Briley swore she could hear each flake as it fell to the earth.

The storm came upon them unexpectedly and with brutal force. A gust of wind swept the scarf from around her neck, leaving one end to flutter. The mare pranced and put her head down against the fierce blowing while Briley frantically searched for any shelter. She climbed down from the wagon and sought out the mare, moving her hands over the animal's back until she reached the bridle.

The shadow of pine trees veered in and out of her vision, but it was toward those shadows that she led the horse and wagon. The snow began to pile up and soon covered the toes and heels of her boots. They reached the copse of thick pines before another gust swept up the freshly fallen snow.

She huddled against the tree, bringing Nessa as close to her as possible. The horse seemed oblivious to the rampaging blizzard and even content to shield Briley from the worst of it.

"**BRILEY!**"

Her body shook. From a shudder? she wondered. No, from an outside force.

"Open your eyes!"

Warm breath caressed her cheek, and she could almost move her limbs again. She felt weightless, and then something cocooned her to block the frigid air she swore would kill her. She heard the man's voice now calling her name over and over. The shouting made her head hurt, and Briley forced her eyes open to see who made her head pound.

"Thank God."

His face a blur, she blinked a few times to bring him into focus. Instead, blackness swallowed her whole.

When her eyes opened again, there was no snow and no cold. Her body lay beneath thick layers of quilts. A fire blazed steadily in the stone hearth, emitting enough heat to wonder why she wasn't sweating. She could see only the black of night outside one of the windows. In the small kitchen stood a large man, his back to her. Briley hefted aside the blankets only to realize she was in her long white nightgown and not the clothes she'd put on that morning.

Every muscle in her body moved slower than usual from a deep ache she didn't have before. *The storm.*

Peyton turned when the bed creaked. He held a bowl in one hand, a spoon in the other. "I knew you were too stubborn to die." He walked toward her and set the bowl and spoon on the small table beside the bed. "How are you feeling?"

Briley looked around the one room of the cabin. "I'm not sure. What happened?"

Peyton pulled a chair from the table and turned it so he could sit and face her. "You don't remember anything?"

Briley studied Peyton, though she looked beyond him as she searched her memory. "I remember hitching up Nessa, that's what I've named the mare, to the wagon and starting for town. The storm came so quickly and I couldn't see. We finally found shelter in the trees . . . that's all I recall." Her gaze met Peyton's now. Dark shadows marred the space around his eyes. His hair looked as though it had been combed only with hasty fingers. His dark beard had thickened since the last time she saw him, but that was only yesterday.

"Emma left this morning to tend another patient, but promised she'd be back tomorrow. She'll be glad to know we won't be having a funeral this week." Peyton lifted the bowl again. "You need to eat this, and if you're up for it, more until you've had your fill—doctor's orders."

Briley didn't reach for the bowl. "What

happened?"

"You nearly froze to death."

Her eyes widened and filled with concern. "Nessa?"

"She's fine. Fared better than you, but then she's used to a strong, Montana winter. By the amount of snow that had accumulated in the wagon, you had to have been there a while."

"Did you find me? How?"

Peyton nodded and held the bowl back out to her. "You eat and I'll talk."

Briley accepted the bowl and began to spoon the thick broth in delicate strokes and waited for Peyton to relay what she didn't remember.

"It was late afternoon, and I came back this way after my weekly rounds of the outlying farms and homesteads."

"You went out in that storm on purpose?"

Peyton's lips formed a half smile. "It wasn't so bad when I left early in the morning. By the time the worst of the blizzard hit, I was more than halfway through my rounds and holed up with Clete until it passed. When I arrived here, it had all but abated."

Confused, Briley stopped eating. "How is that possible? We were stuck under that tree, unable to see anything. The snow never stopped."

"A lot of snow fell in a short amount of time, but the storm only lasted a couple of hours. The temperature dropped, and I imagine you fell asleep without realizing it. It doesn't take long to fall victim to a bad storm out here."

Briley moved aside the bowl and gently laid her hand on Peyton's arm. "Then I owe you my life. Have I been out for long?"

"This is the third day. You had a bad fever the first two days; it broke last night."

"Well." Weakness began to overwhelm her senses, and Briley slipped back beneath the covers. She wasn't going to ask him what happened to her clothes or why he was the one who had remained behind to watch over her. "I've been in some harsh storms before, back in Ireland, but nothing like that. The snow and wind came out of nowhere, and they were fierce."

"With so much land in between homes and towns, it's easy to get lost, and that's what's dangerous out here." Peyton picked up the soup bowl and refilled it from the cast iron pot. He returned and handed it to Briley. "A little more should satisfy the doctor."

Briley managed a small smile and took

the bowl. "I do realize that I have a lot to learn about living on the Montana frontier."

Peyton sat back in the table chair. "I don't know you all that well yet, but this land has a way of bringing out the best and worst in people. You've survived your first storm, and that says something about what you're capable of doing."

Was she capable? Before they left Ireland, Briley might have questioned her own strength. The world had collapsed on her and so many others these past four years, but by a strong constitution, she'd survived. There were times when she marveled on how.

Briley glanced around the cabin. After only a week, it felt more like home than the small flat she shared with her family in New York. Here, memories and ghosts didn't await her in every dark corner. She still met them from time to time in her dreams, but when awake, peace filled her heart and mind much as it had before the war. She'll never know Christopher Smith, the man who would have been her husband, and yet, he'd given her a chance beyond her imaginings.

"Well, I haven't quit yet, Sheriff," she said with a smile. "I suppose it's time to find out just how resilient I am."

BRILEY LIFTED A basket of scones and fresh soda bread from the seat of the wagon. When she began to move around a couple of days after she awakened, it was to find that her cabin was not only clean, but well stocked with more supplies. She suspected Peyton was behind the generosity, and as much as she didn't want to accept charity, she wasn't going to dishonor his kindness by offering to pay him back this time. She'd used a small portion of those provisions to fill two baskets—one for Emma and her husband and one for the sheriff.

Nessa and Briley spent some getting to know each other better the day before. She had even managed to climb onto the mare's back once, and Nessa seemed to have already forgotten the blizzard ordeal. Briley, on the other hand, would not soon forget her carelessness, which could have ended in their death. Out here, she would assume nothing was as it seemed until she learned otherwise, and she had much to learn.

A thin stream of smoke trailed from Emma's clinic chimney into the frosty, afternoon air. Mindful of the ice and snow beneath her boots, Briley held onto the wagon until she could grasp the railing in front of the building. The front door opened before she stepped onto the wooden walkway.

"How wonderful to see you up and around and out for a visit." Emma invited her into the clinic and then shut out the cold. "You've come at a good time. My last patient just left."

Briley followed Emma inside to where a bench sat against the wall. She accepted the doctor's offer to sit down and set the basket beside her. "I hope you like scones and soda bread."

Emma lifted one side of the cloth and inhaled. "They smell wonderful. What's the occasion?"

"A thank you. Sheriff Sawyer—Peyton— told me you sat with me for two days. I know it's your job, but I'm grateful."

Emma smiled. "Thank you for the lovely gift. It is my job, and yet it never feels that way when I'm with a patient or a friend, and you and I are going to be such great friends, aren't we?"

Briley's smile widened. "I would like that." The vise around Briley's heart eased just a little.

AFTER ALMOST HALF an hour, Emma was pulled away by a new patient who had managed to smash his finger with a hammer, leaving the small limb broken. Briley wished the doctor well and quickly excused herself. Rather than walking the short distance to the jail, she opted to drive the wagon. When she entered the jailhouse, she was met with the sounds of shouting and something metal hitting what she assumed was the wall. A man appeared in a doorway from a back room and closed the door. He was no less handsome, standing tall with thick brown hair and kind eyes the same shade.

"You have . . . guests."

He pivoted and grinned. "Not guests, just the Teeter brothers. They're regulars." He walked toward her and glanced down at the basket. "I'd wager a guess that you're Miss Donaghue."

"And you're Mr. Latimer, Emma's husband."

"I am. Pleasure to meet you."

"And you, Mr. Latimer."

"Casey, please." He nodded toward the basket. "Do you want help with that?"

Briley handed him the basket of scones and bread. "It's for Peyton. Emma already has yours."

Casey's grin widened. "Aren't we the lucky ones. Peyton was called away to the telegraph office. He shouldn't be much longer if you'd like to wait."

She hesitated, and then shook her head. "I should return home. I'm not confident enough yet to drive the wagon without full sunlight."

"How are you feeling?"

"You've heard what happened?"

"Peyton mentioned it when he came to get Emma; asked me to watch the jail for a few days."

Briley didn't know what to say to that. Peyton had given up his duties to look after her, which means he'd been there the entire time. She cleared her throat and pointed to the basket on the desk. "If you could see the sheriff gets that, I'd be grateful."

Casey nodded, and seemed to study her. "I sure will, and thank you for our basket as well, Miss Donaghue."

"Briley, please, and you're most welcome." She said her goodbyes and climbed into the wagon. She had one more stop to make before returning home. The shopkeeper at the general store wore her silver hair in a bun atop her head and spectacles perched on her dainty nose. The woman was tall and her back as straight as it might have been in her youth, though Briley guessed her age closer to seventy.

"Maeve O'Reilly at your service, young lady." The woman's warm smile put Briley at ease with the request she was about to ask the storekeeper.

"Briley Donaghue, Mrs. O'Reilly."

"It's Maeve, and what a lovely wonder to hear the voice of my homeland. I've been away so long I'd almost forgotten the sweet sound of the west counties." Maeve ushered her inside and settled her hands on her hips. "Come in, warm yourself, and tell me what I can do for you today."

During their morning visit, Emma was kind enough to recommend the store owner as a possible employer, and Maeve's kindness bolstered Briley's courage. "Do your customers ever have need of a seamstress or dressmaker?"

Maeve's shrewd eyes narrowed. "I can't rightly say. I used to do the fair share of this town's sewing, but these fingers." She held up her hands. "They don't do the fine work they used to without giving me pains."

Briley removed two folded samples from her basket and handed them to Maeve. "I'm a weaver, but I do fine stitching as well."

Maeve held the white cloths trimmed in lace up to her eyes. "Better than fine, dear. These are as pretty of Irish lace I've ever seen. A weaver, you say?" Maeve continued to finger the delicate cloth. "Do you have more of these?"

"A few pieces."

"We'll sell them here in the store, and I'll get you a good price for them, too." Maeve folded the handkerchiefs on the clean counter. "Is your stitching as fine with clothing?"

Careful not to rejoice aloud, Briley nodded.

"We can use a bit of custom finery in Crooked Creek with more folks moving into the area. I've an idea. I'll provide you with the cloth you need for a few items, and then we'll deduct it from your earnings, see how things work out. Does that sound fair?"

Disbelieving at her good fortune, Briley nodded again. "More than fair."

Maeve nodded once. "Good. We'll also advertise your services as a seamstress and bring in a little more business for us both."

Overwhelmed, Briley left the store with some fine cloth and a promise to have supper with Maeve the following week. The drive back to the cabin was eventful as her thoughts filled with new patterns and designs for the cloth, and more importantly, with hope for her future.

She guided Nessa and the wagon to the barn, unhitched the wagon as she'd been shown, and settled the mare into her stall with a handful of grain. She checked the water and then secured the barn door. With her full basket, Briley trudged through the snow to the side door of the cabin.

After stoking the fire, she'd settled at the table with a cup of tea, a scone, and the new cloth, when a knock sounded at the door. A mild breeze swept inside when she opened the door. "Peyton. Please, come in."

Briley waited as he stomped the snow off his boots as he'd done each time he visited her. Had it truly only been a little more than one week since she arrived in Crooked Creek?

"I came to thank you for the scones and bread."

The weight Briley tended to carry with her seemed to lighten whenever he was around. "I'm glad to hear that Casey and the Teeter brothers did not sample too much. I hope you enjoy them."

"Oh, I will." Peyton removed his hat and looked around. "It looks as though I've interrupted you."

Briley glanced at the table. "Not at all. I prefer to keep my hands busy, and the new fabric was too tempting not to look over tonight."

"Mrs. O'Reilly said you'll be doing some sewing for her."

"And for others, I hope."

"It won't be long before she gets word out that there's a new seamstress in town."

Briley watched his fingers as they gripped the edges of his hat. "May I offer you some coffee or tea? I'll have supper ready before too long if you'd like to stay."

"I won't turn down the invitation."

Briley waited while he hung his hat and coat on the pegs by the door and then invited him to sit down at the table. Her small space lacked any other seating besides the bed, but he didn't seem to mind. After three days of watching over her, he likely knew the cabin as well or better than she did.

She handed him a cup of coffee. "I

thought perhaps you might prefer this."

He smiled in thanks and lifted the cup to his lips. When he lowered the cup, his eyes sought hers. "This cabin is becoming rather homey, and now you have new prospects as a seamstress. Does this mean you've decided to give it a go here for the long term?"

Briley joined him at the table and sipped tea from her cup. "I believe I have. May I ask you a question, sheriff?"

"Of course, ask me anything."

"When you decided to return here and become the sheriff, did you regret leaving anything or anyone behind?"

Peyton made himself comfortable in the chair. "My siblings married and scattered. I have a sister in Colorado with her husband—they have a small spread— and I sold mine. I saw how the mining destroyed the lands, and I couldn't be a part of it any longer." He sighed deeply. "When I came here, I had decided on a new life and that's all I needed to know. No regrets, no second-guessing my choices."

"You didn't fight in the war."

He shook his head. "Lincoln's war office wanted what the iron ore and silver mines provided more than they wanted me on the battlefield. Sadly, I believe my contribution caused more deaths than the few bullets I might have fired."

"I'm sorry, I shouldn't have pried."

"It's all right." Peyton was quick to reassure her, and he leaned forward, his arms resting on the table. "No regrets. I don't talk about it much, especially with my family. Casey knows, and I imagine he's told Emma by now, but she's been kind enough not to say anything. I always thought she thought less of me for not joining up with the rest of the men in the beginning, especially after David was killed, but I was wrong."

Briley also leaned forward, closing the distance with only a table between them. "Emma and Hattie are strong women, and I don't believe that those who have lost and moved on with such courage would ever disapprove of anyone who offers so much in kindness toward others. Besides, as sheriff, your life is on the line every day."

Humbled and deeply moved, Peyton reached out and squeezed Briley's hand once before letting go and sitting back. "Then have you made your decision?"

Briley's gold-flecked brown eyes brightened when she smiled. "When my family left Ireland, I held back every tear and my heart ached more and more the farther from home we sailed. When I left

New York, it was to run away from my loneliness, my fears, and every horrible memory of losing my family. What the journey here gave me time to realize is that not all of the memories left me scarred."

She reached out and held her hand palm up, waiting for him to lay his once again in her grasp. When he did, she covered his large hand. "For better or worse, I didn't come west to give up or give in. My life may not have turned out the way I expected or even wanted, originally. However, I believe I'm where I should be. Christopher brought me out here, provided this cabin, and I was still a stranger to him. Hattie and Emma, by their strength and fortitude, have given me the courage to see beyond my own challenges." Her eyes sparkled with unshed tears. "And you saved my life in more ways than one."

"So, you're staying?"

Briley's lyrical laughter filled the interior of the cabin. "Yes, I'm staying."

Peyton's own laughter joined hers. "Then, Briley, I'd like to toast the beginning of a beautiful friendship." Together they raised their cups and drank, smiling over the rims.

Later that evening, after Peyton had left, at ease and comfortable with her surroundings, she pulled the letter from Christopher out of her trunk.

Dearest Briley,

I won't ask you to forgive me, for my choice has left you alone in a strange land. I can't explain why I must do this now that the war is over, but I didn't serve my country the way I hoped. This is my last chance. Do not fear life here. I cannot offer you much, but this cabin, the land, and everything on it are yours. I do not expect to return, nor should you wait for me. The people of Crooked Creek are good and honest, and if you give them a chance, they'll welcome you into their lives.

I would have liked to have known you, and maybe someday our lives will cross. I wrote you out of a selfish desire to not be alone, and marrying me would have left you with an uncontended husband. Your letters gave me the strength to do what I should have done when the war began. I am grateful to you for that.

With the fondest wishes that you find the life you deserve, yours in spirit,
  Christopher

The words held different meaning for her now that the disappointment had evaporated. He hadn't left her alone after all. Fate brought her to Crooked Creek, and here she would build a new life, one unlike she had ever imagined.

THE END

Thank you for reading "Briley of Crooked Creek"!

Scroll through to enjoy "Clara of Crooked Creek," the next short story in the Crooked Creek series.

Clara of Crooked Creek

MK McClintock

She longed for a new beginning. What she found was a place to call home.

No longer willing to allow society's opinion to influence her life, Clara Stowe sought a change, and what better place than the frontier. With her young daughter by her side, she embarks on an unexpected undertaking to the Montana Territory. With grit and determination, they arrive in Crooked Creek to shape the life Clara had always dreamed of and honor the memory of the one they lost.

CLARA OF CROOKED CREEK

Crooked Creek, Montana Territory
May 1866

THE SILVER CREEK EXPRESS stagecoach rolled over rough roads against a backdrop of some of the most spectacular vistas Clara had ever seen. She was no stranger to lush meadows, but the green fields of Connecticut paled in comparison to the thousands of acres spread out on either side of the dusty road.

Her smile widened at the sight of a pair of eagles dancing overhead. Clara's hand pressed against her chest when a herd of horses basked in their freedom as they ran across the abundant fields.

"Mama, look!"

"I see them, Alice." She expertly reached for her daughter before she fell on the passenger opposite them. Clara peeked around Alice to see out the window on the opposite side. Antlered animals, too many to count, moved as one against a backdrop of snow-capped mountains.

"What are they?" Alice asked.

"I believe they're elk. Do you remember the photographs from the book we brought? Tonight we'll take a look."

Alice turned to the man across from him. "Do you know?"

The man's brow shot up in apparent amusement. "Your ma is correct. They're elk." He looked to Clara. "You've come a long way."

"It is that evident?" With a pleasant

smile on her face, Clara smoothed the lines of her gray-and-white striped traveling dress. Gideon had told her it highlighted her smoky blue eyes, though in hindsight, it might be a bit too elegant for their destination. Then again, she had not risked everything and ventured out west to relinquish all holds on her cultured upbringing.

The gentleman's mouth quirked. "Are you headed to Salt Lake City or Denver? Maybe even San Francisco?"

"We're going to Montana."

The man's eyes traveled the length of her, and his face reddened beneath his gray whiskers. "I don't reckon Montana's a place for a lady like yourself. It's a mite different from what I reckon you're used to."

Clara only smiled again and gazed out the window. "I do believe it's the perfect place." She turned her attention back to the gentleman, an older man who reminded her of her father, tall, with a stately appearance and military bearing. His clothes, clean if not a little worn, betrayed him as a man of some means.

"Are you from around here, sir?"

"Jesse Pickett's the name, ma'am. From Missouri, but I've spent a few years in these parts with the army. Missed Montana something fierce when my enlistment ended a few months ago, so I'm going back."

Clara wondered what a man of his age was still doing in the army, unless he served as an officer. "The war has been over for a year, Mr. Pickett."

"Not the war with the Indians, ma'am, or with the vigilantes."

Clara glanced at her daughter, but Alice remained oblivious to the conversation as she continued to watch the passing landscape out the stage window.

"Vigilantes?"

"Nothing to worry yourself over, ma'am." The man also glanced at the young girl and lowered his voice. "The army knows what they're doing."

Clara did not share the man's confidence in the army. Although freedoms had been won and a country remained intact, had they not just lost countless lives? To speak so casually of killing men sent a shudder through Clara's body. She had loved one of those lives taken much too early.

TWO STAGECOACH WAY stations later, and after a night in a log-sided hotel in the growing town called Bozeman, the stage lumbered through a vast valley of spring meadows lush with grass and wildflowers. Alice slept as only a child did, tucked beneath the arm of her mother. Jesse Pickett remained their traveling companion, regaling them with tales of Montana.

"Crooked Creek is a right nice town. Not much too it yet, but I reckon it won't be long before the area changes even more." Jesse started in on another story of mining when the stagecoach picked up speed, jostling Alice awake.

"Mama?"

"It's all right, darling." She looked at their companion whose lips had thinned into a grim line. "It is all right, is it not, Mr. Pickett?"

"Can't rightly say, ma'am. Only two reasons I can think of for a stage driver to run the horses like this, and neither are good." He leaned his head out the window, and the shooting began. He pulled himself back inside. "You hold onto your girl. This is going to be—"

More shots, the sound of panicked

horses, and the sudden feeling of weightlessness as Clara and her daughter tumbled forward.

"Mama!"

Clara's arms surrounded her daughter, protecting her as gravity pushed them from one end of the coach to the next. They collided with Mr. Pickett, but he did not cry out. A torrid pain shot through her spine and another through her leg, but still she did not let go. Alice's cries were muffled by her mother's embrace.

A resounding calm engulfed them as Clara pressed a kiss to the top of her daughter's head and allowed the darkness to carry her away.

"SHE'S COMING AROUND."

Aware of a minor discomfort in her side, Clara tried to ignore the pain and raise her head.

"You don't want to do that yet."

The voice was soft, feminine, and incredibly comforting. She was aware of another presence in the room, wearing the musk of horse and pine-scented air. Clara inhaled, her thoughts drifting back to the first time those same smells drifted into the stagecoach window.

"Ma'am? Can you hear me?"

The man had a voice, a pleasant one that reminded her of Gideon. Her Gideon and their . . . "Alice."

She heard her own voice, weak and foreign. "Alice?"

"She's just fine. You took good care of her." The woman's voice soon had a face to match. Copper-colored hair framed kind features and concerned eyes. "That's right. Come on back to us."

Clara's consciousness returned fully and with it a searing ache on the front of her head. "Where's Alice?"

"Your daughter is fine. You both took quite a spill out there. She's resting now." The woman came into focus. "I'm Dr. Latimer—Emma. You're in Crooked Creek."

"Clara." She pressed a hand to her forehead. "Clara Stowe. I'd like to sit up."

"You can, now that you have your vision back. Gently now, there you go." Emma remained close, but it was the strong arms of a man who helped her up. "This is my husband, Casey Latimer. He and the sheriff found you two days ago."

They had been on the stagecoach, almost to their new home, when . . . the frightful details flitted in and out of her memory. "What happened out there?"

Casey moved to the foot of the bed where Clara could see him clearly. "What do you remember, Mrs. Stowe?"

Clara did not correct his misconception on her married status. "My daughter and

I were in the stage, somewhere after Bozeman." She took a deep breath and strained her ribs in the process. "There was a man traveling with us, a Mr. Pickett. We heard gunfire—I think it was gunfire—and suddenly the . . . we were falling and it seemed as though we'd never stop."

She watched the doctor and her husband exchange a brief glance. "What did happen?"

Casey crossed his arms against his chest, his expression bleak. "The stagecoach was ambushed. After the drivers were killed, it appears the horses lost control and the coach detached."

"The coach toppled somehow, didn't it?"

Casey nodded. "There was a hill near the road. The coach didn't roll far, but enough to cause some damage. You and your daughter are lucky, Mrs. Stowe.

Very lucky."

"Please, it's Clara." Clara attempted to calm the pounding in her head. She looked to Emma. "You're certain Alice is all right?"

"I promise. A few bruises, but you protected her well."

"You said she's resting."

Emma held Clara's wrist and then pressed the end of a stethoscope to Clara's chest. After a few seconds, she nodded and stepped back. "She is now. You've been out for two days, but we've kept her occupied. She's been sleeping most of the time, which is what she needed. When she wakes again, I'll bring her in to see you."

"Can't I go to her now?"

Emma shook her head and with a firm, yet gentle touch, kept Clara from rising. "You weren't as lucky as your daughter. You'll be fine, but I need to monitor you for a few days. Nothing is broken, but you have a rather large and unsightly bruise on your back and another on your leg. Can you move your toes?"

Clara preferred not to consider what she'd do if she could not walk out of this room on her own two feet. She closed her eyes and moved her toes. "It hurts, but they work."

"The pain is most likely from the compression on your lower back. The pressure should ease in a few days, though I'm afraid the pain will linger."

Casey drew her attention. "Peyton— that's Sheriff Sawyer—will want to talk with you when you're feeling up to it."

Clara nodded and accepted a cup of cloudy liquid Emma handed to her. With a hesitant glance at the doctor, she swallowed half and pushed the cup away.

"I need you to drink it all."

With a grimace, Clara swallowed the

remaining liquid and handed Emma the empty cup.

"You'll feel drowsy soon. Your body needs rest in order to heal itself."

Clara nodded and then looked to Casey. "Do you know who did this?"

"Not for certain." Casey relaxed his arms and shared another look with his wife, who nodded once. "There's been some trouble on the stage lines caused by a small group of riders. Before two of them were captured last month, they numbered six—four white men, an Indian, and we believe a woman."

Clara shuddered. "I didn't see any of the riders. Mr.—wait, you said my daughter and I were lucky. What about Mr. Pickett?"

"I'm afraid he didn't make it."

WHEN CLARA OPENED HER eyes

again, night had overtaken the day. One of the windows in the room had been left open a crack to allow fresh air to circulate in the room. A gentle shift of the bed brought Clara's head around where she peered into a pair of light brown eyes. "Hello, my darling."

"I waited and waited. I was a good girl."

"Yes, you were a very good girl." Clara opened her arms and waited for Alice to snuggle against her side.

"Are you hurt?"

"I'm all better now that you're here."

Emma entered the room carrying a tray laden with food. "Good to see you awake, and you have your color back." She lowered the tray onto a table and walked to the bed. "And I see our other patient found you. Alice and I have become friends, haven't we, Alice?"

The little girl nodded and offered up a small smile. Emma held out her hand.

"Your mother has a visitor. How would you like to help me downstairs while they talk?"

Alice look to her mother. "Can I?"

Surprised at Alice's ease in the company of a stranger, Clara nodded. "Of course you may. You listen to Dr. Latimer."

Alice giggled. "Her name is Emma, like my doll."

Clara returned the smile. "Yes, it is."

Alice slid off the bed and slipped her hand into Emma's. As they departed, a man entered, tall and rugged with blond hair mussed by his hand after he removed his hat. His striking blue eyes were made even more brilliant by skin darkened from the sun. "Mrs. Stowe."

"You must be Sheriff Sawyer."

Clara watched as the sheriff carried the tray from the table to the bed and helped her situate it on her lap.

"Call me Peyton. Most folks around here do."

"Then it's only fair for me to tell you that I am not Mrs. anyone. I'm simply Clara."

Peyton's quick nod indicated he understood, yet he passed no judgment. "I've spoken with your daughter. She's bright and eager to help."

Clara found she could still laugh. "Alice takes after her father in that way. You've come regarding the accident."

Peyton nodded. "Casey relayed what you already told him, and I'm afraid I don't have much more to tell you. I just wanted to be sure that you and your daughter are well."

"We have Dr. Latimer to thank for our good health, and I'm told you and her husband. How did you find us?"

"When the stage didn't come through as scheduled, we rode out. Casey's what you might call an unofficial deputy when I need him."

Clara straightened the spoon on the tray but made no move to raise it or sample the fragrant soup. "Mr. Pickett— the gentleman in the coach with us—I'm told he died."

Peyton shook his head. "He was gone when we got there, except it's him I came to ask you about."

"Oh?"

"He told you his name was Jesse Pickett, correct?"

Clara grew curious at Peyton's tone. "He did. He also said he was coming here."

"Did he say what his business was here?"

"Mining, though I only half-listened. We traveled in the same direction for a few days." Clara straightened the best she could. "Did you know Mr. Pickett?"

"I did not, but there is a family not far from here by the name of Pickett, and I'd like to be sure of my information before notifying them."

"I'm sorry, but he didn't speak of family, only mining and soldiering."

"I appreciate your help." Peyton stepped closer to the bed. His eyes held concern and he glanced over his shoulder as though expecting someone to walk through. "Do you plan to stay in these parts?"

"I've bought a house here, and it's my plan to open an inn."

Peyton's eyes narrowed. "I heard tell of a man from Connecticut purchased the big house that used to be owned by the miner, Mr. Cromwell."

"Yes, my father purchased it on my behalf, but I assure you I have the paperwork in order. I am the rightful owner."

Peyton held up his hands and smiled in a way that eased Clara's troubles. "I'm not questioning you, and it's not uncommon. I had thought at first it might be your husband."

Clara felt as though the words she wished to confess lodged in her throat, and she could do nothing to release them.

"It's no one's business. You'll find Crooked Creek is a good and understanding community with plenty of strong-minded women." He grinned. "It takes gumption to come out here on your own. I imagine you'll do just fine."

TWO DAYS LATER, EMMA announced that Clara was fit to leave the clinic. Clara eased into the last of her clothing and faced the doctor. "I can't thank you enough for what you've done. Especially for taking such good care of

Alice."

"Well, it's my job, and I can't take all the credit for Alice. Briley, that's Peyton's wife, has been teaching your daughter how to sew."

Clara was equally skeptical and surprised. "Alice, sewing? She's only five years old."

"A very bright five years."

Clara nodded. "She could read at age three, and loves to sketch, but she showed no interest in sewing when my grandmother tried to teach her." Of course, Clara thought, it wasn't the activity but rather the company. Although Clara knew how her grandmother felt about both Clara's life choices and having an illegitimate child, she had doted on Alice the way a grandmother should, and for that Clara was grateful. Still, her grandmother had been a strong member of the community, and society wasn't as forgiving. "I'd like to thank Briley for her kindness, though I'll admit nothing sounds better than home right now."

Emma walked with Clara down the stairs to the main room of the clinic. "I hope by home you mean Crooked Creek."

Clara stepped outside where Alice sat on a bench with another woman, presumably Briley. "I do hope so."

Alice saw her mother and slid off the bench to her feet. "Look what I did!" She held up a bit of what appeared to be a scrap of fabric. An uneven line of stitches ran across the length of the cloth.

"You've done a wonderful job, darling." Clara's eyes rose to meet the other woman's when she stood. "You must be Briley."

The woman's rich brown hair matched her eyes; her smile was warm and genuine. "Briley Sawyer."

Her musical voice surprised Clara. "You're Irish, as is my grandmother. She and my grandfather came over from Donegal."

"A truly lovely place. You'll find there are a few of us around these parts." Briley folded a square of white fabric and placed it in a basket on the bench. "My husband tells me you've purchased the Cromwell house."

Clara nodded. "I haven't seen it yet, but if it's as the banker described, then I intend to turn it into an inn."

Briley's brown eyes gleamed. "What a joy it would be for this town. Though, I daresay we don't get too many visitors."

"I wouldn't suspect so, way out here." Clara indicated the basket. "May I look at what you just put away?"

Briley smiled when she handed Clara the handkerchief, though she was too quick to dismiss her own talents.

"This is fine work." Clara turned the cloth over in her hands. "The finest I've ever seen. My grandmother brought beautiful Irish lace back with her, but she couldn't manage stitching this delicate."

"Briley pulls a finer thread than anyone I've seen," Emma said.

Clara looked up from the fabric. "If you have more, I'd like to see it."

Surprised, Briley said, "The mercantile carries some of my work, and I've a few pieces at home."

"I would love to purchase some for the inn." Clara eased off the boardwalk as a wagon pulled around. She reached for her daughter's hand before she realized the driver was Casey Latimer.

Casey lifted Clara's bag into the back of the wagon while Emma kept a bracing arm around Clara's waist. "I'd rather you take it easy for a few more days. Casey will drive you home, and I'll check in on you this afternoon after I've seen to a few patients."

Casey lifted Alice first onto the seat of the buckboard. "You sit right there in the middle and you'll have the best view." Alice giggled and sat down with a little bounce. He helped Clara step onto the wheel and held her arm to steady her until she was seated.

Briley stepped up next to Emma and the wagon. "I'd like to come along with Emma this afternoon if you don't mind."

For the first time in five years, Clara meant it when she said, "I'd like that."

CASEY HELPED CLARA EASE down from the buckboard, and to Alice's delight, swung her through the air before lowering her to the ground.

"Can we do that again?"

He carried Clara's bag into the house

and set it down in the foyer.

"We brought your trunks over—they'd been sitting at the sheriff's office while you were unconscious. I'm afraid two of them were damaged and everything rifled through. Did you have any valuables in those trunks?"

Clara shook her head and walked farther into the house, Alice's hand in hers. "Nothing that can't be replaced." Except Gideon's watch which she had carried on her person and had not thought of until now. She turned to Casey. "There was a silver watch pinned to my dress."

The look on his face told her what she suspected. "I'm sorry, but they took everything of value."

"Will the bad men find us here?"

Clara started to bend forward, the lingering pain in her side making it impossible to finish. Casey knelt on the wood floor in front of Alice.

"No one is going to hurt you or your ma again."

Alice swayed from side to side and considered. "Good. He smelled bad." She wrinkled her nose and with a small grin spun away from her mother.

"Alice, wait."

The girl stopped mid-skip and turned. "Yes, Mama?"

Clara's voice shook when she asked Alice to return to her side. Casey still knelt on the floor, his expression one of unease. "Alice, what do you mean the man smelled bad? Did you see him?"

Alice bobbed her head and then shrugged her small shoulders.

Casey gently laid his hands on those shoulders and repeated Clara's question. "Did you see the bad man, Alice?"

"Yes. He won't get us again, right?"

Casey exhaled on a slow, deep breath

and smiled at the girl. "No, he won't."

When Casey rose, Clara's eyes met his. She wanted to ask him to send for the sheriff, to send for anyone who could keep her little girl safe. "Alice, why don't you explore the house a bit?" She quickly added, "Stay where I can hear you, darling."

When Alice skipped into the great room, Clara turned to Casey. "If this man knew Alice saw him, he probably wouldn't have left her alive."

"Not likely. I promise you'll be safe. I'll tell Peyton, but you don't need to worry. This is a quiet town—most of the time— and we look out for each other here."

Clara believed him, and she wasn't going to allow a single fear to turn her away from their new home. She did not fool herself into believing life on the frontier would be as easy as living on her parents' estate, but she didn't come west because it would be uncomplicated. She brought her daughter here to live a dream, and they would live it.

"The way I see it, we should have died when the stage rolled. I can't imagine coming that close to losing Alice again." Not after losing Gideon, she thought.

Casey nodded in understanding. "Alice will be safe, too. You have my word."

BY THE TIME CASEY had checked the house and made sure Clara's trunks and bags were within reach, which meant she wouldn't have to lift anything, the morning had turned into midday. Alice was napping on the settee in the parlor where Clara could keep an eye on her. She now stood in the foyer of the grand house, admiring the craftsmanship in the few pieces of furniture the previous owner had left behind.

She saw the cavernous space as it would be once she filled it with comfortable sofas and chairs, carefully selected end tables, beautiful lamps, and paintings throughout. Even the small details like Briley's beautiful, hand-sewn linens and the watercolor miniatures her parents collected from their travels, would help to make the inn feel more like a home.

Clara walked through the spacious great room, dining room, a kitchen large enough to cook a feast, a parlor, and what appeared to have been a study. A small room off the kitchen served as the laundry. She ventured up the wide staircase to the second level where four large bedrooms—all semi-furnished— offered varying views of the glorious landscape.

She made her way up the second staircase to the third floor where three bedrooms and a cozy sitting room filled the space. The furnishings had come with the price of the home, and though the previous owner had left behind only beds and a few pieces of furniture on the first and second floors, they would make do until what she ordered had arrived.

She ran her hand over the curve of a headboard and smiled. The memory of Gideon on their first night together before he left for the war floated to the surface.

They may not have all of the conveniences of home . . . no. Clara had to stop thinking of Connecticut as home. Their life was here now. Crooked Creek was home.

She returned to the main level and checked on her daughter who still slept. Alice would be hungry when she awoke. Clara was a fair cook when the occasion called for it, though she planned to hire someone far more skilled for the inn. A soft knock at the front door drew Clara out of the parlor and into the foyer where she welcomed Emma and Briley inside.

Briley kept watch over Alice while Emma examined Clara's wounds. "I had hoped to find you sleeping when I arrived. Casey told me what Alice said."

Clara fastened the front of her dress and moved to make tea. "I don't have much to offer you except tea, and I have a tin of biscuits we brought with us." Clara put the kettle on the stove, then turned back to Emma. "My arrival in Crooked Creek was planned meticulously, and I daresay, an ambush was not part of my plan." Clara glanced toward the kitchen door when she heard soft laughter and lowered her voice. "If anything had happened to Alice, I wouldn't forgive myself. She's all I have."

"I remember when I came out here with David, my first husband. He didn't want to stay, but I did. All manner of things went wrong our first few weeks here, but this place and these people are worth the effort." Emma sidled closer to Clara. "You won't leave, will you?"

Clara shook her head without a moment's thought. "I have no intention of running away when faced with a challenge, especially not on my first lucid day." They shared a laugh and quieted when Alice walked into the kitchen with Briley close behind.

"Mama, look!" Alice held out a delicate doll made of fabric scraps. It should have looked haphazard, but the deliberate blend of colors created a beautiful pattern. A small symbol was stitched on the dress, covering the doll's heart.

"It's lovely, darling." Clara looked at Briley. "You made this?"

Briley nodded. "I brought a few in this morning for the store."

Emma leaned in to look. "I haven't seen these before, Briley. What a fantastic idea. What is this over the heart?"

"'Tis a Claddagh. Friendship, love, and loyalty." Briley's eyes glistened with unshed tears. "My mum taught me when I was young."

"It's a precious gift." Clara handed the doll back to Alice. To Clara's surprise, Alice wrapped her arms around Briley and whispered, "Thank you."

THE WOMEN VISITED WHILE Alice's new doll made friends with the doll she'd brought from home. Emma excused herself. She had an appointment with a patient and once again asked Clara to rest, promising she would check on her tomorrow.

Briley remained, though she'd grown quiet watching Alice.

"Is something wrong?" Clara poured more tea into Briley's cup.

"No, sorry." Briley nodded toward the girl. "She reminds me of my sister. We lost her to a fever whilst still in Ireland."

"I'm so sorry." Clara's gaze drifted to her daughter. Nothing more precious on the earth existed for Clara. "I can't imagine. I didn't have siblings."

Briley turned back to her new friend. "I had a brother. He was older, stronger, wiser, and I loved him dearly."

Clara didn't want to ask, but the same loss she experienced when Gideon died echoed in Briley's eyes. "The war?"

Briley nodded and wiped a tear from her cheek. "He and my father both. My father made it halfway through the war and died at Gettysburg. It wasn't his fight, or Michael's, but they believed in the cause."

"And Michael, your brother?"

Briley drew in a deep, shuddering breath. "He was killed at Appomattox. A friend who fought alongside him delivered the news himself when he returned to New York."

Clara reached across the table and covered Briley's hands with her own.

"I don't speak of it often," Briley confessed. "Peyton knows, of course. I have so few reminders of my life before coming here, but Alice . . . it's good to remember."

Clara squeezed Briley's hands, a gesture of comfort, though she wondered how anyone who had suffered such loss could find relief. No amount of good will had helped Clara overcome the sadness of losing Gideon. "I lost Alice's father to the war. He died at Leesburg." Clara looked over at her daughter who had fallen asleep on her blanket, holding both dolls. "Two months after Alice's birth. He never knew he was going to be a father."

Briley turned her hands and held Clara's. A special and unbreakable bond formed between the two women in that solemn moment.

"Did your family approve of you coming west?"

Clara leaned back then and laughed, though she heard the exhaustion in her own voice. "It wasn't about their approval. You see . . ." she glanced again at Alice and said quietly, "Gideon and I weren't married."

"I see."

Clara sensed Briley's gaze on her and looked back. "We had planned to marry, the war began, and Gideon wanted to serve. We were foolish enough not to question if he would return, but he gave me Alice before he left."

Briley did not look upon her as a woman bearing the mark of a sinner but rather as a new friend whose well of compassion would never run dry.

CLARA WOKE THE NEXT morning to a glimpse of sunlight as it filtered through the bedroom window. She'd left it open the night before with the curtains pulled back to allow fresh air to fill the room. Her family used to go on holiday once a summer to the ocean, and she loved the crash of waves against the rocks and beach. However, the invigorating salt-water air couldn't compare to the purity of what now filled her lungs. With the scent of pine on every breath, and the air crisp and pristine, she paused to inhale deeply.

She reached for her robe at the end of the bed and slipped into it as she ventured across the hall to her daughter's bedroom. Alice had been excited when she saw the large bed in what was to be her new room, though Clara would need to add some feminine touches for a young girl. With Alice still deep in sleep, Clara washed and dressed, then made her way down the stairs to the main level. She opened the back door off the kitchen, pressing a hand against her side when she extended too far. Wincing, she wondered how long the bruises would pain her, and at the same time, she counted her blessings . . . poor Mr. Pickett.

A dim light cast colors through the morning sky as the sun crested the mountain peaks. Alice would sleep for another hour yet, and she had work to do.

She made use of the lavatory—hadn't Alice been surprised when she realized they didn't have indoor plumbing in Crooked Creek—and washed up at the basin in the sink. She mentally planned out the four bedrooms she would use for guests, and a thrill of excitement coursed through her. They didn't need the funds a small inn would bring, but she was determined to be useful, to prove her ability to survive on her own and support a child. Her grandmother's hurtful words of doubt and how her granddaughter needed a husband echoed through her thoughts before Clara could stop them. Why would a woman with everything she could ever need or desire, want to trade in her privileged life for one in the wilderness? Clara quickly pushed the unwanted question aside because she already knew the answer. It's what she and Gideon would have done together.

Clara heard a knock at the front door. When she entered the foyer, the pounding ceased, followed by a low whimper, scratching, and a hoarse plea for help.

She opened the front door an inch to see outside. A dog thumped its shaggy tail against the wood, laid down, and whimpered. The animal wasn't alone on the veranda. "Good heavens."

THE YOUNG BOY'S WEIGHT, though slight, was more than Clara could handle on her own. She managed to help him into the parlor, where the only furnishings were a settee and end table. She eased him down, pausing when a soft moan escaped the boy's lips.

Clara spun around when she heard the patter of stockinged feet on the floor. "Alice, come here please."

The young girl hurried to her mother's side, her honey-colored hair half loose and half in a braid.

"Can you do something for me?"

The little girl nodded and then turned

at the sound of another whimper. "Puppy!"

"Yes, a puppy. Now Alice, can you stay right here and keep the puppy and this boy company?"

The girl's eyes widened in question, though instead of voicing fear, she bobbed her head, lowered herself to the ground, and rested a hand on the dog's head. Clara spared a glance to the boy and rushed to the kitchen. She unearthed a bowl and pumped water, though precious little came out. She lifted the hem of her petticoat, slid it across the edge of the table until it tore, and rent the fabric to create two cloths.

Back in the parlor, Alice still sat on the floor, the dog's head resting in her lap. The boy's face appeared paler somehow, but Clara could not see any visible injuries. "You did well, Alice." Aware of her daughter's nearness, but unwilling to send her into another room at the moment, Clara dampened one of the makeshift cloths and smoothed it over the boy's head to wipe away the dirt. A few small scratches appeared.

"What's wrong?"

"I don't know, sweetheart." The boy needed a doctor, but Clara couldn't leave him alone or alone with Alice while she fetched Emma. She moved aside his clothing the best she could but saw no blood. "I need you to come with me please." With Alice's hand in her own, Clara moved them quickly to the front door that had remained open. "Alice, stay right here in the doorway where I may see you."

"Yes, Mama."

Clara lifted her skirts and ran down the steps. A wider road leading into town crossed with the one to the house. She spotted a man riding away from town, but she had little choice. "Excuse me!"

The man turned and rode back to where she stood. He wore clothing similar to those of Casey and Peyton, except for the strange leather boots he wore that appeared to mold to his skin.

"Mrs. Stowe?" The man was without hat, but he nodded once. "Carson White Eagle, ma'am. Emma mentioned you to my wife." He looked behind her, no doubt seeing both the open door and Alice. "Is everything all right?"

"No. Please, Mr. White Eagle, I need some help."

Carson needed no other information. He dismounted, secured his horse, and followed Clara inside the house. She led him to the parlor where the boy had remained laid out on the settee, unconscious. "He was at my front door this morning. I don't see any injuries, but he needs a doctor. I had no way to take him. Is Emma in town?"

Carson nodded. "I just rode by there. She's been at the clinic all night with a patient. Casey and my wife are there with her, too." He knelt in front of the boy and with great care and efficiency, moved his hands up and down the boy's legs and over his arms. "I don't feel anything broken." Carson gently lifted the boy into his arms.

"Alice, stay here please and watch over the puppy, will you?"

Alice smiled in reply while Clara followed Carson outside and to his horse.

"Can you manage him for a minute?"

Uncertain, Clara nodded and allowed Carson to transfer the boy into her arms while he swung up into the saddle. He took the boy's weight from her. "Don't worry about the boy, Mrs. Stowe. Emma will take good care of him."

Clara watched as Carson rode away

from the large house nestled in the pine trees, the boy safe in his arms.

ALICE DIDN'T UNDERSTAND what had happened, only that a young boy not much older than herself was hurt and he had a puppy. She had refused to leave the dog's side, which made dressing her more difficult. The dog surprised Clara by remaining behind when Carson rode away with the boy. Once Alice was dressed, it was still early for breakfast. Clara hoped the small eatery she saw in town was open, but first, they'd check in at the clinic.

They walked to town with the puppy in tow. As much as Clara appreciated Emma and Casey leaving her a horse and wagon until she purchased her own, she would need lessons in both harnessing and driving. She continued to marvel at the vast differences between the East and the grand wilderness of the great West, which despite the influx of adventure seekers, miners, and cattlemen, managed to retain its glorious beauty.

A few heads turned as they passed storefronts and a few wood-sided houses. Clara smoothed the front of her gray silk dress, though she knew it to be unwrinkled. The cool morning required little more than the square shawl for comfort. By a few of the thorough gazes sent her way, Clara suspected that the new wardrobe she had commissioned before her departure would be of little use to her in Montana. She knew the more convenient dresses with fastenings in the front would be necessary since she left her maid behind, but they were still the latest fashions. Ignoring the onlookers' questioning gazes, she smiled and continued to the clinic, all the while listening to Alice's excited questions about everything in sight.

"What's that?"

Clara stopped at the edge of the boardwalk in front of Emma's medical clinic. Her gaze followed her daughter's to an expansive meadow surrounded by thick trees, though Clara wasn't able to tell the difference between the various types of pines. Clara would be able to teach Alice everything she might have learned from a governess or tutors back in Connecticut, but her knowledge of their new surroundings was lacking.

She noticed only a small building, half erected, on the edge of town before the meadow opened up.

"It's the new schoolhouse, or it will be soon." A woman with light blond hair covered by a wide-brimmed hat sat atop a tall, gray horse. The woman dismounted and a pair of brilliant green eyes met Clara's. "Sorry if I startled you."

Clara returned the warm smile with one of her own. "You rode up without a sound."

"Lots of practice." The woman held out a gloved hand. "I'm Hattie White Eagle."

"I'm Clara Stowe, and this is my daughter, Alice." Clara accepted her hand and studied the woman. "I believe we've met your husband, Carson." Clara quickly went on to explain. "A young boy stumbled upon my doorstep early this morning and your husband was riding nearby. He brought the boy to Emma."

Hattie nodded toward the clinic. "In that case, I'll join you. You're already well-known in our little town."

Clara helped Alice skirt around a puddle of water in the road. "Is that so?"

"Not many people survive an accident like you did."

Clara preferred not to think about how

close she and Alice had come to losing their lives. "We were lucky. Have you lived in Crooked Creek long?"

Hattie nodded. "My husband and I—my first husband—started a ranch a few months before the war broke out. No place else has ever felt like home, so I stayed."

Clara considered the confident woman beside her and wondered if she would be able to allow herself to love again. Perhaps she found it more difficult because Gideon had not been hers in every way. She had lost the man she loved and the father of her child, but she hadn't lost a husband.

"Are you all right?"

Clara turned to Hattie who watched her with curious eyes.

"Yes, just thinking how strong a woman must be to live out here on her own. I don't know how you or Emma managed for so long." Clara released a breath with soft laughter. "You don't know me, and I don't mean to speak of such personal matters."

A brief touch of Hattie's hand on her arm stopped Clara, but it was Hattie's next words which brought her comfort. "You've come this far on your own, and anyone with the gumption to do that is stronger than they might think."

Clara watched Hattie secure her horse to the hitching post in front of Emma's clinic and step onto the boardwalk. "Why don't we see about the boy you found."

Alice turned to her mother. "Is he going to be all right?"

"I do hope so." Clara smiled at her daughter and stood next to Hattie who rang the silver bell hanging outside the clinic door. "We've brought his friend along to say hello." She indicated the dog who stood by Alice's side.

It was Carson who opened the door rather than Emma.

"Hattie, Mrs. Stowe."

Hattie's husband brushed a hand over his wife's arm in a simple and natural action that Clara envied. "Please, it's Clara. We've come to look in on the boy, if we may."

Carson nodded toward a closed door on the far wall. "Emma's with him upstairs now. She said he'll be fine. Exhaustion and hunger seemed to be the cause."

Hattie removed her hat and loose strands of wavy, blond hair fell to her shoulders. "I'd better see if Emma needs any help." She exchanged a brief look with her husband, one that spoke of an immediate understanding shared by those who knew each other well. "Clara, I hope we'll have more time to talk again soon." She leaned forward to meet Alice at eye level. "It was very nice to meet you,

Alice. If it's all right with your mother, I'll teach you how to ride a horse someday. Would you like that?"

Alice giggled and nodded. Hattie rose, tweaked Alice's nose, and disappeared behind the door Carson indicated earlier.

Clara guided Alice to the narrow bench along the wall and cautioned her to remain seated. She turned back to Carson. "I want to thank you for your help this morning. Your timing was fortuitous."

When Carson smiled, it reached his brilliant blue eyes. With the exception of a healthy tan from the sun, his heritage appeared no different than hers.

"I'm just glad the boy's all right. Must have given your little one a fright."

Clara glanced at Alice. "She's stronger than she looks and more worried about the boy . . . I'm sorry, do you know his name?"

Carson shook his head. "He was still unconscious when Emma scooted me from the room and only came down once to fill me in on his condition. As far as I know, the boy hasn't spoken yet." Carson's eyes drifted back to Alice. "Have you had breakfast yet? You probably haven't had a chance to stock up on provisions."

"It's early yet for breakfast. We'll go after . . ." She glanced at Carson when he chuckled. "Have I said something wrong?"

"Not at all, just your mention of the early hour. Bess—she and her husband run the small café—are open before the sun. Most folks around here get an early start."

Heat creeped into Clara's face. "We're accustomed to a different way. That is, breakfast was set for a specific hour. I suppose it will take more than a change of wardrobe to fit in."

"Nothing wrong with the way you look." He glanced at the door when they heard movement on the other side, then continued when the door remained closed. "My wife tells me you're opening up a hotel in that big house. I figure this town could use with all the refinement it can get."

"Thank you, Mr. White Eagle."

"Just Carson." He pulled a small wooden horse from his pocket and handed it to Alice. "A 'welcome to Crooked Creek' gift."

Alice's eyes brightened. "For me?"

"Sure is."

"That's a beautiful horse, Alice. What do you say?"

"Thank you, Mr. White . . . uh."

Carson chuckled. "Carson's a mite easier."

Alice responded with a grin and turned

her attention to the intricately carved wooden horse.

"That's very kind. Thank you."

Carson shrugged. "I like to keep my hands busy. Finished that one while I was waiting for news on the boy. Who's your friend?" He reached out and rubbed the dog's ears. For his part, the animal wagged his tail and pushed his head into Carson's hands.

"He was with the boy, though he hasn't left Alice's side since. I'm not sure Emma would approve of him being inside."

"She's a stickler for cleanliness, but I'm sure she'll make an exception this once." Carson gave the dog another pat and then rose.

The door to the stairway opened and Emma stepped through. Her crowded waiting room didn't appear to surprise her. "Clara, I'm glad you've come. You've brought company."

Clara laid a hand on Alice's shoulder. "The dog belongs to the boy. I thought perhaps it might help to see him."

"His name is Mason, that much I managed to get out of him. Except, he did say the word 'bandit' twice. Perhaps that's his name."

The dog perked up and thumped his tail against the floor. Rather than admonish them for bringing the dog into her clinic, Emma patted the puppy's head with her free hand. "Mason's sleeping again, but I'm sure he'll be happy to see Bandit when he wakes." Emma carried a bowl of water to the back door and tossed the contents onto the spring grass. When she returned, she stumbled, the bowl falling from her hands. Carson caught her before she hit the floor. The bowl didn't fare too well. Alice's worried cry echoed Clara's silent one as she rushed to the doctor's side.

"How long has it been since you've slept, Emma?" Carson asked, his voice tight and filled with concern.

"I have two other patients upstairs who needed tending." She righted herself with Carson's help, but both he and Clara remained close. "I'm fine, I promise."

Clara looked around the tidy clinic and wondered how Emma managed on her own. "Do you have anyone to help?"

"A good nurse is difficult to find, let alone another doctor in these parts. I manage pretty well . . . most of the time. Hattie knows a little about tending cuts and wounds, and Casey saw enough during the war to help." She smiled and took in a restorative breath.

Carson didn't appear convinced of his friend's ability to manage on her own, but after assuring him again that she was fine, he relented and stepped away. "I better go and help Casey and Peyton search for the boy's family." Carson grabbed his hat and exited the clinic.

Emma sat beside the young girl and tapped the wooden horse. "Are you going to name her?"

Alice looked at the horse and then at Emma. "I have to think about it."

Emma bit the inside of her lip to keep from grinning at Alice's serious tone over the importance of the wooden horse's name. "A wise decision. Such a horse should have a special name." Emma patted her hand and rose to stand by Clara.

"You have a way with her, as do others in this town." Clara lowered her voice and kept a close watch on her daughter. Bandit stretched out on the floor beside Alice. "She's always been a vivacious child, curious about everything. Alice isn't old enough to understand why people weren't kind or why she could not play with other children her age."

Emma covered Clara's hand with her own. "Her father?"

"Gone before he knew, before we had a chance to marry." The words, quiet and reserved, were not easy for Clara to say.

"She's a happy and healthy child. You've done well, Clara, and don't worry what people here might think. I spent most of my life in the East and came from a family not unlike your own."

"You're saying people around here won't judge us?"

Emma didn't answer immediately, and when she did, Clara appreciated her honesty. "Some will. It's the way of things, and times haven't changed enough for an unmarried woman with a child to be free of ridicule, but you'll find that most people in our little town will care more about the person you are than some of the . . . choices you may have made."

Clara released a slow breath and cast a loving gaze upon her daughter. "I can't quite say why this soon, but I feel as though I've found a home here. A place where Alice and I can make a new life, build something that will stand for all time, a legacy."

Emma began folding bandages, listening to Alice's soft voice in the background as her doll and new horse talked with each other. "Do you plan to do it alone?"

"Didn't you?"

"For a time." She set aside the first pile and stared on the second. "I wasn't sure I'd marry again, or love again, but when Casey came along my heart didn't give me a choice."

"I loved Alice's father very much. I'm not ready to love another again, not yet."

"There's plenty of time." Emma placed

the folded white bandages on a shelf and returned with a tin and a bottle of clear liquid. She dropped various silver instruments into the liquid. "I learned early on that if I keep all of my surgical equipment disinfected not only before a surgery, but ongoing, it prevents infection." Emma laid out a fresh white cloth and one by one removed the instruments. "I say there's time, but we both know that's not always true. Neither of us had enough to love our men, but when it comes to matters of the heart, we can't be timekeepers."

Clara nodded and glanced at her daughter who appeared to have ended the conversation between the doll and horse. "Gideon and I were childhood friends before we were suddenly something more. But for now, I cannot consider courting when I have a daughter to raise and the inn to open."

"I expect you'll do well on both counts."

"Yes, well, I'm afraid I'll be in need of a new wardrobe and a lot of help."

Alice rose from the bench, the doll and horse tucked beneath one arm. "I'm hungry."

"We'll go to breakfast, and then perhaps some shopping at the general store."

Alice's head bobbed up and down in agreement.

Clara turned back to Emma who spoke first.

"I disagree about you requiring a new wardrobe. It's been a long time since I've worn the latest fashions; they aren't practical for what I do, but you'll be running this town's first hotel. You might need a few everyday dresses for the work, but I imagine your guests will appreciate a hostess in all her finery. I certainly would." Emma finished cleaning the instruments and tucked those away in a velvet-lined wood box. "As for the help, what do you need?"

"I need to hire a cook and servers when I open the rooms and dining room, but a cook now. Two women to help with the cleaning and laundry, and someone who can help with repairs around the place."

"Sounds as though you'll need more than just a few people. Are you ready for that?"

"I have . . ." Clara looked down at her daughter who seemed quite intent on the conversation. "My father was generous."

"The town could certainly use another good employer."

Clara interpreted Emma's brisk nod as approval for her plan. "Might I post an advertisement somewhere? I'd like to hire locally, if possible."

"There are plenty of good people who could use the work. Mrs. O'Reilly—she prefers to be called Maeve—at the general store will know who's been looking for work. She can also help you out with any new clothing you need."

"Thank you." On impulse Clara walked around the exam table and hugged Emma. "For everything."

THEY ENJOYED A hearty breakfast at Bess's café before making their way to the mercantile. Bess had even taken a plate of scraps outside for Bandit. The dog meandered along beside them but stopped at the threshold of the general store and sat. He seemed content to wait for them outside, though it took some gentle maneuvering to convince Alice.

Maeve O'Reilly was not what Clara had expected in a shopkeeper in Montana. In truth, she didn't know what to expect, but a woman close to her grandmother's age with a ramrod straight back and beautiful silver hair gathered atop her head was not it.

"Briley Sawyer is our seamstress in town. Not a lot of call for new dresses, but there isn't anyone with a finer hand at stitching." Maeve pushed her spectacles back in place when they fell too far down her nose.

"I've met Briley. I plan to buy some of her work for the inn and commission a few pieces. She does lovely work."

"None lovelier in all the territory." Maeve brought out a small pad of paper and a pencil. "I'll be sure to tell Briley you're looking for new dresses—five you say, how about that—and she'll come by for measurements and such."

"That would be fine, thank you." Clara watched Alice walk across the store to a short shelf of books. Her own library of volumes her father was shipping out wouldn't arrive for a few weeks. One of her and Alice's greatest joys was reading together before bed, but she'd only brought a few of Alice's favorites. "We'll be looking at your books, and I could do with some provisions." She reached into her pocket. "I've made a list."

Maeve studied the piece of paper with the neat lettering. "A few items we'll need to order from Denver, but we'll get you everything. I can fill this and my grandson can deliver everything when he returns."

"I would be grateful, thank you." Clara added a few bills to the counter.

"This is too much." Maeve scooted half of the bills back.

"Please, put it on account as a deposit toward the dresses."

"I like you, Mrs. Stowe." Maeve slipped the money into a box and closed the lid. "Now, let's have a look at the books."

Alice had already picked out two from the shelf when the women joined her.

"Those have some mighty big words for a little girl."

"Alice reads quite well, even on her own."

Maeve peered at the girl. "How old are you?"

Alice held up one hand. "Five years. Mama says I'll be six years soon."

"Five years and already reading these big books? I'm quite impressed."

Clara nodded, swelling with pride for her daughter. "She has a gift for it."

"She's a mite young to be going to school, but I expect she'll fit in well enough."

"You have a school?"

Maeve nodded and carried the books they'd picked out to the counter. "They're building a new one on the edge of town. We have a new teacher, and not many students, but the town is optimistic more will come."

OPTIMISM WAS EXACTLY what Clara needed. No matter the challenges she'd faced, she and Alice had found a new home, and she would make it work for them both. They'd stopped at the clinic after the general store, but young Mason was asleep again after consuming only a small bowl of broth. Emma concluded that it had been quite a while since the boy had a decent meal. Clara thanked God and her parents for not turning her out when she confessed what she and Gideon had done. Even though they'd been old enough to understand the potential consequences of their indiscretion, love prevailed. The romance of war turned out to be far less romantic than anyone ever anticipated.

It was two hours before they made their

way back home. They left the store with three new books and a few sweets for Alice. Clara had posted her advertisement on the store's board since the town lacked a newspaper, and Maeve had promised to send any prospective employees to the house. She caught herself and smiled. No, the inn, she thought with determination. The top floor of the grand house would be their personal residence, and the rest would be an inn. Clara admitted that her skills did not extend to running a business, but she'd been taught how to run a household. The rest she would learn. Alice would have a home filled with people who wouldn't judge either of them.

Clara's parents had hosted dinners and entertained guests on numerous occasions, until their friends had learned the truth relating to Alice's illegitimacy.

They had discovered that Gideon's mother, who had refused to accept Alice as her granddaughter, had made it known that in no uncertain terms did Clara and Gideon have a child. Her heart ached whenever she remembered the woman's cruelty. Gideon had been one of the kindest and most generous men she'd ever known. His father had attempted to soothe the discord and welcome Alice into their lives, but the damage had been done. Society was unforgiving.

Her own parents had accepted the situation, though not without disappointment. They knew Clara's heart and loved little Alice unconditionally. However, as long as Clara's grandmother scorned Alice's birth for the scandal it caused, Alice would never have the life she deserved. Until now.

ONCE CLARA HAD tucked Alice in for her nap, she made lists of what she would need for each room. Most of the furnishings and accessories would be ordered from the East or one of the larger cities in the Midwest. She would inquire about local craftsman to build tables and chairs for the dining room. She planned to offer her guests both comfort and elegance.

A knock at the front door reminded her to add a smaller bell to her list, one guests could ring upon their arrival. Casey stood on the other side of the door, dust-covered and grim. He removed his hat when she asked him to come inside.

"May I get you some coffee?" Clara studied his bleak features.

"Thank you, but I won't be long. It seems you deserve to know what we discovered seeing as how you saved the boy's life."

Confused, Clara said, "Emma saved Mason's life, not me."

Casey nodded. "There was a small camp two miles south of here on the creek. Not much to it except a wagon and a few belongings. We found the boy's sister and mother, both half-starved and . . . tied up. It's a wonder the boy escaped and made it this far."

"Will his mother and sister live?"

"Emma's with them now. Beyond that, we don't know."

Clara's hands tightened into fists, though she didn't know why. She forced herself to relax. "I hope you've arrested someone."

"We have. The boy's father and an older brother. They looked healthy enough and well-fed, like they hadn't been to the camp in a while. They also had a few bags of gold on them." Casey rubbed the edge of his black hat. "It appears to be a portion of the gold from the stagecoach you rode in on."

"I wasn't aware the stage carried gold. Only a portion?"

Casey nodded. "This particular group of outlaws hasn't ventured this far north before and may have brought the boy and father in to help. Most of the gold is still missing."

Clara looked up toward the ceiling where Alice slept three floors up. "Alice said she saw one of the men from the accident."

"Don't worry yourself about that. We'll do our best to get them to talk. I'd as soon leave your daughter out of this, and she may not remember as much as she thinks. It's hard enough for an adult to remember much in the face of fear."

Clara relaxed. "She's bright, and I have no doubt she'd remember. However, I do appreciate you leaving her out of this.

She's been through too much already."

"She seems to be happy and settling in. She's young yet and may not be ready for school, though that's a question for Miss Patterson, the town's teacher." Casey managed a small grin. "I suspect Alice will have no trouble catching up with kids much older."

Clara returned the smile. "No, she won't. Where might I find Miss Patterson?"

"At the old schoolhouse. A fire a few months back destroyed the classroom. We're building a new one in the meadow, but for now you can find her most days in the church. She's holding classes there for now."

"I appreciate your help and for letting me know about Mason's family."

"You're part of this town now, and we help our own." Casey replaced the hat on his thick brown hair and stepped outside.

She stopped him before he stepped off the porch. "Does this sort of excitement happen often around here?"

"It's as quiet of a town as you can find in the West."

Casey didn't give her a direct answer, but it seemed it was the only answer she was going to get.

He swung up on his horse and turned toward her. "And Clara?"

She faced him, waiting.

"Don't discount what you did for the boy. You continue to think quickly on your feet, and you'll make a fine Montanan."

SILENCE FILLED THE LARGE house like a heavy weight. Since their arrival, Clara had found comfort in the quiet and stillness. Tonight, with the moon's glow illuminating the room and the night air motionless, the silence became a deafening reminder of their isolation.

Clara calmed her fearful imaginings. She would grow accustomed to the peace of her new surroundings. She pushed the bedcovers away, slipped into her robe, and walked across the hall to where Alice slept. Her chest rose and fell with steady breaths. Her doll and the horse Carson had given to her were nestled on the pillow beside her. Bandit was curled up at the foot of the bed while his soft whimpers told Clara he was dreaming. She walked across her daughter's room to gaze out the window. The moon cast its light across the land, driving away shadows here and creating others there.

Chiding herself for the useless worry, she returned to her bedroom. She heard a low growl before a hand snaked around her waist and another covered her mouth. Menacing words followed foul breath as the man spoke against her ear.

"Where's the gold?"

She shook her head to indicate she didn't know. The man squeezed harder. Her only thought was for Alice. She shook her head again and tried to pull away from his grasp, to no avail. The growling increased, this time closer.

"I ain't asking you again, lady. I saw the lawman come here after he took the gold. You tell me, and I'll let you and the pretty little girl live."

Fear turned to fury when he threatened Alice. With all her strength, she pulled back his fingers until they bent into an unnatural position. He slapped her and she kicked, forcing him to the floor in agony. Bandit clamped onto the man's leg. It bought her enough time to race back to her daughter's room. Alice was on the verge of waking. Clara closed the door, sent up a prayer, and ran down the stairs. She heard the man following her and hoped he would continue to do so.

Dread returned when the stranger caught up with her and tripped her. She fell and slid across the foyer floor. Before she could regain her footing, he hauled her up against him.

"Your girl will live if you tell me where the lawman took our gold."

"I swear to you, I don't know." He pressed the knife against her side. "He said most of the gold wasn't there, and the other men from the robbery must have it."

Clara heard a whimper from upstairs followed by her name. She couldn't go to her daughter. Her only hope was to keep him away from Alice.

The man spewed a string of filth from his mouth and pushed her toward the front door. "Open it."

Clara did as told. She would go

anywhere if it meant keeping him away from Alice. The moonlight had dimmed in the last few minutes, and the subtle shift in nature saved her life.

"Drop!"

She closed her eyes, loosened her body, and fell to the porch. One of them stepped on her leg before she managed to roll out of the way. The scuffle didn't last long. She heard a loud thud and felt the porch vibrate. A pair of strong arms lifted her to her feet.

"Did he hurt you?"

Clara looked up at Peyton. "No." She said it again with more conviction. "No, we're all right. Is he . . . dead?"

"Not yet." Clara spun around to see Casey hefting another man—this one much smaller—onto the back of his horse.

"You sure you're not hurt? Look at me, Clara."

She faced Peyton and tried to calm her accelerated heart. "I'm sure. They were after the gold."

Peyton picked up his hat and proceeded to tie the hands of the man he felled. "We caught another one trying to sneak into the clinic."

Suddenly mindful that she wore only her nightclothes, Clara secured the edges of her robe. "Were they the men from the camp?"

"No. We got the father to talk. He and his older son helped these men rob the stage you came in on. It seems the father and son took all of the gold. Carson is riding out to get it now." Peyton dragged the man to his feet, ignoring the moans. "I need you to go back inside now. You and Alice are safe."

"Peyton, wait. How did you know they'd be here?"

"We didn't. Their partner told us. He

was young and scared and foolish enough to try and go after the family." Peyton handed his prisoner off to Casey and faced Clara. "You should know, it was the older son Alice saw the day of the accident. He saw her, too. No harm will come to her."

Clara didn't wait for the men to leave. She closed the door and rushed upstairs to find her daughter. Alice sat on the floor in the hall between their bedrooms, Bandit's head in her lap. A soft moan escaped the dog, and Clara knelt down beside them.

"Mama? What happened to Bandit?"

"It looks like he hurt his leg." Clara choked back her relief and pressed a kiss to Alice's cheek. "Why don't we make him comfortable, and tomorrow we'll see if Emma can fix him?"

"Can we sleep with you? We had a nightmare." Since her daughter still clutched her doll, she assumed the "we" also included the toy.

"Yes, for tonight. I think Bandit should stay with us, too." Clara gently lifted the dog into her arms and carried him into her room. She would worry about clean linens tomorrow. Bandit curled up at the foot of Clara's bed, and Alice climbed beneath the covers. Once the girl was settled, Bandit gingerly scooted toward her, resting his head on her covered legs.

CLARA AND ALICE returned to the clinic the following morning after breakfast at Bess's café. She needed the comfort of people and noise. Alice had asked questions regarding the night before, believing what she heard had been a nightmare. However, her primary concern was for Bandit, who to Clara's surprise, had jumped from the bed without assistance. Still, she insisted Bandit see the doctor.

The door to Emma's clinic stood open. The doctor sat at her desk looking over a thick book.

"I hope we're not disturbing you."

Emma glanced up and then closed the text. "Of course not. I'm researching unusual symptoms a patient came in with earlier." She tweaked Alice's nose and lowered herself to the girl's level. "Mason, the boy you helped save, is getting better. He's awake now, and I'm sure he'd like some company. Do you and Bandit want to come upstairs?"

Alice tilted her head back. "May I?"

"You may. I think Mason would like a visit."

Alice turned back to Emma. "Can you fix Bandit's leg first?"

Emma knelt down next to Bandit. "How did he get hurt?"

Alice shrugged. "Mama said he was a really good puppy, and he's happy now. He was sad before."

Emma glanced up at Clara. "I see." She ran her hands up and down the dog's legs. "It doesn't appear anything's broken. He might just have a little bruise."

"He'll get better." Alice's words conveyed an innocent confidence found only in the young.

"Yes, he will. I think Mason would like to see Bandit now." Emma reached for the girl's hand and said to Clara, "I'll be right back. Hattie is up there now with the boy—she's giving me a hand today. Alice will be looked after."

Clara nodded and watched Emma escort her daughter upstairs, smiling as she listened to Alice's cheerful chatter. Clara walked to the open door and looked out to the street. Spring had settled like a soft blanket of sunshine over the town.

"Your girl is a treasure."

Clara turned at the sound of Emma's voice. "Yes, she is, and she's taken with you. You'd make an amazing mother."

Emma's hand slid over the top of her flat belly. "I do hope you're right. Casey and I will want to borrow Alice for the practice."

Clara's eyes welled. "A baby." She remembered the fear, the excitement, the worry, and the joy she experienced the day she learned she'd become a mother. "Congratulations."

"Don't go crying or you'll get me started." Emma laughed and wiped a hand over her eyes. "I've decided I want a daughter just like your Alice. A little girl would be nice. Then again, I'd be happy with a boy who looked like his father."

"Then they'll be the best of friends, even with the years between them."

Emma stilled. "You're staying for good then. I worried you might have second thoughts after this mess, but Casey told me that New England women don't scare easily."

"He was speaking of you."

Emma nodded. "And of you and Briley. Hattie's been here the longest, but she's not from these parts either. We've all been touched by tragedy and heartache, and we'll carry those memories for the rest of our lives, but it's our adversities which have brought us all here, made us stronger."

Clara tugged the edges of her floral shawl closer together. "I would give anything to have him back. Gideon would have been a wonderful father. Alice is so much like him— strong, beautiful, with a good heart."

Emma stepped toward her friend. "Alice is like you, Clara. You are all of those and more. You'll always have a part of her father, and you'll see him whenever you look at her. I remained in the cabin David and I shared together because it was all I had left of my life with him. When Casey stumbled through my door, I realized there was enough room in my heart for David's memories and my love for Casey."

Clara walked to the narrow bench and lowered herself onto it. "I'm not strong enough yet, but I will get there. I believe that now."

Emma sat down beside Clara and wrapped an arm around her shoulders. "You will be."

Clara didn't share Emma's optimism when it came to her own heart, except she had moved on—her journey to Crooked Creek, a new home, a business, and now new friends. She'd moved on more than she had realized. Clara faced her friend.

"What's going to happen to Mason's mother and sister? I suspect his father and brother will go to jail."

Emma's sigh sounded like one of regret. "Casey told me not an hour before you arrived. Susan, Mason's mother, and Ellen, his sister, will be all right, and of course, they'll have Mason. There are no charges against any of them. They were the ones abused, though I'm not sure yet what will become of them."

"Where will the men go?"

"I don't know. The nearest army fort or prison I would imagine." Emma rose and walked to her desk. "It's unlikely they'll see their family again."

Clara's choices since she first asked her father to buy the stately house in Crooked Creek, Montana Territory, had been based on impulse and a desire for a new and exciting life. She saw no reason to stop following her instincts. "When they're well enough, I'd like to hire them."

Emma crossed the rooms, absently lifting a bottle of powder from a shelf. "Hire who?"

"Susan and Ellen." At Emma's quirked brow, Clara continued. "I'm hiring staff for the inn, and there's no reason why they can't hire on, if they choose. There will be plenty of work to go around. I'll pay a fair wage and the inn will be a place where they can be proud to work."

"Clara, you haven't even met them yet."

Motivated to take the next step, Clara rose from the bench and grinned. "Why don't we remedy that?"

SUSAN AND ELLEN Reed would need weeks of nourishment and rest before they would be fit to help at the inn. Those weeks would give Clara the time she needed to hire the remaining staff and order the remaining furnishings and sundry items needed to properly run a refined hotel in the West.

Susan and Ellen both cried when she offered the jobs. Clara would need to find them a place to live in town, and their wages would see to it they could live in relative comfort. Their lives would be different from this moment forward, much like Clara's.

Alice and Mason bonded over a small wooden horse she gifted to her new friend and decided to share Bandit. When her daughter returned downstairs with Briley without the new favorite gift in her hands, Alice said someone else needed it more. It was something Gideon would have said.

Clara sat on her front porch with a cup of tea after tucking Alice into bed for the night. A gentle breeze blew the trees and brought with it a song of spring. The creek for which the town was named meandered behind the house, and in the quiet night, Clara could hear the water rushing over smooth rocks as the tall grass swayed with the light wind.

She wrote to her father that evening. She told him of their new home, which she decided to call the Stowe Family Inn, a sentiment she thought Gideon would have appreciated. Clara told him of the town and the people she had met thus far, and how Alice had already made new friends. She left out the tale of the survival after the stagecoach crashed and of the unexpected visit from the miscreants, of course. Above all, she thanked him for making their new life in the majestic and wild Montana possible.

When Alice had asked about her own father and why he couldn't be with them, Clara held her daughter close and told her of a brave young man who fought gallantly and gave his life for the people he loved most. It was time for him to join the angels, remaining forever in their hearts. Alice had liked the idea of her father as an angel watching over them from high above.

Gideon filled Clara's thoughts with every beautiful memory she carried in her heart. She could hear him at times whispering words of love and dreams. He would not want her to remain alone—this she knew in her soul—but for now, he joined her as the quiet, moonlight evening enveloped her in peace.

THE END

Thank you for reading *The Women of Crooked Creek*!

Don't miss out on future books.
www.mkmcclintock.com/subscribe.

If you enjoyed this collection of stories, please consider helping other readers by leaving an online review. MK loves to hear from readers, and they may contact her through her website.

WHAT'S NEXT *for* CROOKED CREEK

A NOTE FROM THE AUTHOR

I've been asked by many readers about what is in store for this series, and if there will be a continuation of Clara's story. "Emma of Crooked Creek" was originally going to be the only story, which meant this series came as a bit of an unplanned surprise for me. One thing led to another and there were too many extraordinary women who deserved their own stories. Thus was born *The Women of Crooked Creek*.

I'm pleased to say that there are three additional Crooked Creek installments planned. The next installment is Clara's full story and the introduction of a new hero for her. You'll once again meet all of the main characters from the short stories along with many of the townspeople. The new stories will be written in between other previously-planned projects.

I am as anxious to share them with you as I hope you are to read them. You can always keep updated with what's coming next via my website: mkmcclintock.com. I also post book updates via my blog and social media.

WANT MORE?

Montana Gallagher Series
Gallagher's Pride
Gallagher's Hope
Gallagher's Choice
An Angel Called Gallagher
Journey to Hawk's Peak
Wild Montana Winds

British Agent Series
Alaina Claiborne
Blackwood Crossing
Clayton's Honor

Whitcomb Springs Series
"Whitcomb Springs"
"Forsaken Trail"
"Unchained Courage"

Short Story Collection
A Home for Christmas

You may find all these and more, and see
what's coming next, at mkmcclintock.com.

WRITING AS MCKENNA GREY

The Kyndall Family Thrillers
"Blade of Death"
The Dragon's Staircase
Shadow of the Forgotten

Second-Chance Romance
"Christmas in Moose Creek"
"McKensie's Christmas Gift"
Christmas in the Rockies

ABOUT THE AUTHOR

Award-winning author MK MCCLINTOCK is devoted to giving her readers books laced with adventure, romance, and a touch of mystery. Her novels and short stories take you from the rugged mountains of Montana to the Victorian British Isles, all with good helpings of daring exploits and endearing love stories. She enjoys a peaceful life in the Rocky Mountains where she is writing her next book.

If you'd like to know when MK's next book will be out, please visit her website and blog at mkmcclintock.com, where you can sign up to receive new release updates.

Made in the USA
Coppell, TX
05 September 2020